For Patricia Marley, going to school this year was not a simple task. It meant crossing town on a regular bus for the first time. It meant harder classes and newer faces—white faces. Pat Marley, an irrepressible fifth grader, is Negro and very much aware of the fact that she, together with a handful of other Negro children, will be integrating a previously all-white school. But Pat is not the crusading type and doesn't really want to be part of the new and frightening situation. This is about that year in school and what Pat learns about herself—and others.

Patricia Crosses Town

Alfred A. Knopf   *New York*

Patricia Crosses Town

BETTY BAUM

Illustrated by Nancy Grossman

L.C. Catalog card number: 65-21561

THIS IS A BORZOI BOOK, PUBLISHED BY ALFRED A. KNOPF, INC.

TO MY GRANDCHILDREN:

Julie, Dena, Laura, Jonathan, and Sharon

My affectionate thanks to:

Molly and John Price for steering me in the right direction;

Rae Ollie Dudley for awakening my heart and opening a door;

Virginie Fowler for leading me through it successfully;

Kenneth Donn, my nephew, whose youthful viewpoint and vigilance helped me avoid many pitfalls;

my daughters Sheila Salmon and Marian Sevransky on two counts—they read and reread valiantly and, in addition, were intelligent and farsighted enough to marry Bob and Paul who are knowledgeable in the area of human psychology and thus able to test my ideas;

and my husband Iz for his advice and his faith.

Patricia Crosses Town

chapter 1

It was a biting cold day at the end of March when registration for open enrollment began. Pat's temper suited the day. She kicked an empty can across the street with deadly accuracy. Her best friend, Johnny Meadows, watched.

"What's the matter?" he asked. "Aren't you glad to be getting out of old P.S. 27?"

Pat jammed her chin into her skimpy collar. "Why should I be? I'm in fourth grade and I have friends and I like it here." And she started to run.

Jo-Jo caught up with her and met her eyes squarely. "Lucy Mae's father is a teacher. He ought to know. He told my mother that P.S. 100 is the best school on the open enrollment list. And he told your mother, too."

Pat, when her eyes failed to quell his excitement, suddenly pretended a rush to get to school.

Jo-Jo ran with her. "My ma says if that school is good enough for Lucy Mae Oliver, it's good enough for me," he protested. "Why don't you want to go across town on the bus every day? It'll be fun—you and Lucy Mae. . . ."

"Jo-Jo Meadows, you're. . . ." She searched for a word and settled for a look that mingled disdain and pity. "You believe everything anybody tells you. Everything. And it's not the bus I mind," Pat continued coldly.

Jo-Jo tugged at her arm, trying to slow her up. "Your ma going to register you today?" Pat paid no attention. She walked rapidly, her head down. Then Jo-Jo said carefully, "Say Pat, what's it going to feel like . . . you know . . . seeing white kids all around us every day?"

With one of her sudden expansive smiles, Pat spread her arms heavenward, books and all, and in a voice remarkably like Mrs. Oliver's, she said sweetly, "Like a cloud. We're going to float along and everybody is going to pretend the black ones just aren't there."

"Pat, if I weren't looking at you, I'd say you were Mrs. Oliver talking to the P.T.A. meeting."

A shadow reflected Jo-Jo's feeling of guilt. "Pat, you oughtn't make fun of people. Especially nice ones like the Olivers. They have their own house on our street, and they don't act uppity."

Pat really liked the Olivers—even Lucy Mae— but she didn't trust them. Why would anyone as well off and as light-skinned as they were bother with her family? Mr. Oliver was a school teacher and Mrs. Oliver had been a social worker. Why would they care what happened to her father, who was the handy man in the building they lived in, or her mother, who did housework for people who lived across town. On Tuesdays and Fridays, Pat's mother was somebody's maid and Pat hated to think about people ordering her mother around.

Pat felt confused. She and Jo-Jo usually agreed on things. She stuck out her lower lip. "I don't like Lucy Mae. I don't like her mother talking to my mother and making me go to another school next year." She started to pound Jo-Jo's arm. She wanted him to agree with her.

Jo-Jo pushed her away. "You stop hitting me, now. They're nice people."

Pat suddenly felt ashamed and let him slow her down. She put out her hand. "Truce, Jo-Jo."

He shook his head doubtfully, then took her hand. He was her friend. She had never before had as good a friend. Why couldn't he understand that she had to stay in her own school. She tried again to explain her fears.

"Jo-Jo, tell your mother not to get you a transfer. Then maybe my mother won't get one for me."

"But why?"

"I'm scared. My father told my brother Carl that oil and water don't mix. That's why black people and white people don't mix."

"You just said the white kids will treat us like clouds."

"Jo-Jo! Now I'm serious." She looked at him with tears in her eyes. "My pa said it won't be too bad for Lucy Mae because she's the color of caramel kisses. And she's smart, too. But you and me—look at us. I'm pure black like my father. Jo-Jo, we haven't a chance of keeping out of fights in that new school. And they'll say we're too black to learn anything."

Jo-Jo's eyes opened wide with worry. "If we have fights, do you suppose the white kids' gangs will have real guns? Vanessa's brother said he saw one once."

Pat shrugged her shoulders. Jo-Jo never failed to get sidetracked. Now all he could think of was gangs and guns. As they approached the school, Jo-Jo began to run. "Lucy Mae, wait," he shouted as he ran. He called back to Pat, "Hurry. We'll ask Lucy Mae. Maybe she knows about the gangs."

Without pausing, Jo-Jo kept yelling to the girl who was entering the schoolyard. "Lucy Mae. Does your mother know about the gangs? My mother and Pat's are coming to transfer us today, but we better find out about the gangs—have they got guns?"

Pat brushed past Jo-Jo and Lucy Mae and the other girls. "Big mouth," she whispered loudly to Jo-Jo as she went into the building.

The satisfaction she got from Lucy Mae's blank stare and Jo-Jo's scowl was sorry compensation. She hated herself for her rudeness and her sharpness. *What makes me act that way,* she asked herself. But the only answer she found was in the pretty picture Lucy Mae had made as she stood near the door dressed in a bright blue plaid coat and hat. That girl's got everything, Pat told herself as she dashed to take her own place on the class line.

The classes formed their lines in the large inside yard. The fourth grade stood in the middle, one class next to the other. Pat brushed several children as she got into her place behind Vanessa. She didn't say a word, lest the tears break loose from under her lids.

Vanessa looked inquiringly at her but kept her peace. When Jo-Jo came into the yard with Lucy

Mae, Vanessa nudged Pat. "Have a fight with Jo-Jo?"

"Because I live in his building and my father is the janitor, I don't have to be friends with him." Pat kept her eyes glued to her notebook. She didn't dare look at Lucy Mae.

The whistle for quiet blew and Pat looked up. Mrs. Dillon, Pat's teacher, was on duty. Her class would stay in the yard until all the other classes had gone upstairs. Jo-Jo had slipped into the boys' line and had sidled as close to Pat as he could. "I'm not a big mouth. Did I say. . . ."

"Johnny Meadows. Step out of line. Did you hear that whistle?" Mrs. Dillon came towards them, her flat heels clicking across the cement floor. Each step was a twin of the last; her trim tweed skirt, two inches longer than the fashion, was part of her military appearance.

Jo-Jo stepped out of line. Pat jumped to his side. It had been her fault that Jo-Jo had talked. "I was talking to him," she declared to Mrs. Dillon.

"Then the two of you stand in front of the lines until I can take care of you." Mrs. Dillon went back to her station near the staircase. "Those two," she said aloud to Lucy Mae's teacher. "Impossible!"

Pat was unable to resist a quick imitation of Mrs. Dillon's walk and a titter broke out among the children left in the yard. Mrs. Dillon whirled about quickly and stared at Pat. She continued talking to Lucy Mae's teacher. "The girl, Patricia, has talent. She's a mimic if ever there was one. Too bad she can't use her talents more constructively!"

Class 4-1 went up and Mrs. Dillon kept her eyes on Pat until Pat felt her scalp begin to itch. When only class 4-6 was left in the yard, Mrs. Dillon spoke to Pat and Jo-Jo.

"Well, what have you to say for yourselves? Don't you know that a whistle means SILENCE?"

Pat kept her face blank. Mrs. Dillon's voice rang in her ears like a gong. Mrs. Dillon's grey hair brushed neatly back from creamy skin made her blue eyes seem like bits of steel aiming for Pat's heart. Her hair was the sleek gun barrel, and the eyes were the bullets.

To stop her thoughts, Pat blurted out, "We were talking about the open enrollment. Johnny's mother and mine are coming to school today," she said defiantly.

Mrs. Dillon smiled dryly. "Do either of your mothers think that a new school can help you? Johnny? Maybe. Without Patricia egging you on and putting ideas in your head, maybe you would stay out of trouble. But you, Patricia! How many times have you been sent down to the office this year alone? How many times has your mother had to come and see Mrs. Arnold, the principal?"

"I don't mean to do anything bad," Pat muttered. "It's just for fun."

"But school is for learning, not playing. In gym, instead of playing the games I teach you, you go making up some silly game of notebook relay tag or some other nonsense!"

Pat was silent. She couldn't tell Mrs. Dillon that all the children in the class liked the games she made up on the spur of the moment.

Mrs. Dillon blew her whistle again. "That's enough. On line." When the class was in order, she turned to Pat and Jo-Jo. "Since your mothers are coming to school, perhaps you had better go to the office and wait for them. If Mrs. Arnold asks why you are there, tell her what you did this morning and she will take it up with your mothers. Now, go."

As they walked towards the wide doorway which led to the main office, Pat heard Mrs. Dillon say to the class, "If Patricia thinks she can get away with more in another school than she does here, she is sadly mistaken. It's a wonder I keep my sanity with her in the room."

Pat put her sweater over her arm. "Why are teachers always so mean?" She led the way into the office, and stood still in amazement.

The office was filled with people. People were coming and going out of Mrs. Arnold's room. People were standing in line talking to each other and calling out to Mrs. Oliver who seemed to be everywhere at once.

One woman asked Mrs. Oliver over the heads of several others, "Mrs. Oliver, my husband thinks we ought to be careful and not send our kids where they're not wanted."

Mrs. Oliver answered firmly, "No one wants his child's feelings to be hurt. I don't want Lucy Mae's feelings to be hurt, but we have to take that chance."

Pat poked Jo-Jo in the ribs. Even Mrs. Oliver wasn't sure that Lucy Mae wasn't going to have her feelings hurt. And Lucy Mae was as light-skinned as could be. "Hear that?" she asked Jo-Jo.

Jo-Jo leaned over and whispered, "Lucy Mae told me that the school *does* want us. Her mother went there to see. The principal makes speeches all the time and they have assemblies about us and everything."

"Parrot!" Pat said, not having any other comeback. "As if Lucy Mae knows everything."

"Her mother told her. Mrs. Oliver's been to the school three times. So there!" Jo-Jo was triumphant. His face glowed.

But Pat's fears wouldn't go away. "Maybe the principal wants light Negroes, like Lucy Mae." Just then, Pat was grabbed by the elbow.

"Patricia Marley, you are a disgrace." Pat's mother held on to her. "I just stopped to talk to Mrs. Dillon. She told me you were fresh and disorderly. What are we going to do with you?"

"Don't send me to another school," Pat begged. "Please Ma, I promise to be good. Honest."

"Stop whining." Mrs. Marley whispered fiercely. "You even got Johnny in trouble. If Mrs. Meadows wasn't a fine woman, she'd give you a piece of her mind."

"Then let Jo-Jo go to another school, but let me stay here."

Mrs. Marley held Pat's elbow tightly. "Listen to me. Your pa and I decided to put you in school across town and, by my soul, you're going there. Mrs. Dillon and all your other teachers say you are smart and, before next year, you're going to prove it. Hear me?"

Pat didn't care if everybody heard her. She cried out, "Please Ma, I'm scared!"

"Scared of what?"

"Teachers make fun of me," Pat argued. "Ma, let me stay here."

"Why? Johnny and Lucy Mae are happy to go

across town. They appreciate the sacrifice their parents are making."

Pat pulled until her mother's ear was level with her mouth. "They're not as black as I am," she whispered.

chapter 2

"Is that you, Pat?" a gentle voice asked, and Pat faced around swiftly. She didn't want Mrs. Oliver to know what she was saying or thinking.

"My Pat is worrying," Mrs. Marley answered, and put her wide hand across Pat's back. Pat snuggled close. Her mother's touch was tender. Slowly, Pat began to hate herself for her fear, for her stubborness. Her parents loved her. They wanted her to get ahead the way the Olivers wanted Lucy Mae to get ahead.

"It's your turn to see Mrs. Arnold," Mrs. Oliver said. "After you sign the paper, wait in the auditorium. When everyone is finished, Mrs. Arnold will talk to the mothers and children about next year. Want to wait with Lucy Mae?" she asked Pat reassuringly. "Jo-Jo's going to wait with her. Why don't you?"

Pat glanced in the direction Mrs. Oliver was pointing. Through her lashes, she saw the pretty picture Lucy Mae made in her blue dress with its great big bow. Pat shook her head and sat down on a bench against the wall.

"I'll wait here for my mother," she answered politely, while in her heart she hoped she could get to be as pretty and as smart as Lucy Mae. Only, she knew the hope was useless. She shut her eyes, squeezed her lids as tight as tight could be, and prayed.

"Please, either make me pretty, or make something happen so I don't have to go to school with white children. Please. Please. Please," she repeated long after her mother was at her side, transfer in her hand.

For the rest of the school year in her old school, Pat worked harder than she ever had. She plagued her mother constantly by asking, "Ma, if I make good marks, can I stay in my own school?"

Her father would tousle her hair, saying, "Good marks are their own reward!"

Her report card at the end of the year was the

best she had brought home. All subjects were marked "Fair" except one—behavior. That was still "Unsatisfactory."

"Mrs. Dillon has hated me since she found out about the transfer," Pat said.

Her mother clucked and answered, "Nonsense. How about all the other bad conduct marks you got in other classes?"

"That," said Pat with fervor, "proves all teachers hate me and I might as well stay in this school as any other."

Her mother seemed to have a deaf ear to all of Pat's promises and threats. "You'll like the school fine when you get there," Mrs. Marley reasoned. "And you've got all summer to get used to the idea. Right now, get busy with the dishes. . . ."

And that's how the summer began.

Most of the time, Pat forgot about the transfer. Summer was for fun and there was no time to think about school.

Early in August, the Olivers came back from vacation, and Jo-Jo began going across the street to their house to be coached in reading.

"Mrs. Oliver says you should go over, too," Mrs. Marley said one morning. "Better learn as much as you can this summer." And, despite Pat's reluctance, Mr. Marley walked her across the street and handed her over to Mrs. Oliver.

"Pat doesn't have to read with me unless she wants to," Mrs. Oliver said. "She and Lucy Mae can sit out on the porch and play parchesi or talk."

"Thank you, Mrs. Oliver," Pat's father said, as he looked at his daughter's blank face. "Pat's stubborn sometimes, but she's real smart."

Mrs. Oliver laughed and agreed. "Don't worry. She'll be fine."

After he left, she brought lemonade and cookies out to the porch. "The three of you play parchesi until I finish the dishes," she said.

Jo-Jo poured a tall glass of lemonade at once. "Mind your manners," Pat whispered, and kicked him secretly.

"Ouch, quit it, Pat," Jo-Jo said. "Why are you always picking on me?"

Pat sat bolt upright. She was hurt. What made Jo-Jo say that in front of Lucy Mae? "If that's the way everyone feels, I won't transfer across town," she said sharply.

"Oh, no," Lucy Mae said with a gasp. "Please don't say that, Pat. I'm counting on you. I don't want to be the only girl."

"Your mother said the kids will be coming from all over," Jo-Jo corrected. "She says girls and boys will be transferring from a dozen schools all over Queens and Brooklyn."

The light-skinned girl looked from one to the other. "I mean . . . the only girl from here. I've never been to another school . . . all my friends. : . ."

Pat watched the brown eyes fill with tears and, for a moment, she understood. She put her hand out, intending to touch Lucy Mae's shoulder, but the contrast made her drop her hand fast.

"What have you got to worry about? You're almost white yourself," Pat said bluntly. "With me, it's different."

"Don't keep saying that," Jo-Jo said, standing up and almost knocking over the pitcher of lemonade. "My mother says Negroes are Negroes. Light or dark."

"Please come across town with Jo-Jo and me," Lucy Mae said in what was almost a wail. "Maybe they'll put us all in the same class. I hope so."

Pat stared at Lucy Mae huddled in the big chair. "If you're scared, why are you going? You have the best marks in this school—what do you want to change for?"

"Because," Lucy Mae said pleadingly, "my father says we *have* to mix with white children. Get to know them. Let them know us. That way, he says, we'll learn to understand each other."

Pat shook her head violently in disagreement.

Jo-Jo gave her a meaningful look. "Mr. Oliver is a teacher, and he says—"

"I know he's a teacher, and you don't have to tell me what he says. I've heard it before," Pat said. "But, if I can make my mother tear up that transfer, I'm going to do it."

"But Pat," Lucy Mae said eagerly, "there is a dramatic club in P.S. 100. And you're the best mimic in school. I bet you could be in the dramatic club and in all the plays."

"First of all, assembly plays are corny," Pat said slowly. "Who wants to be in one of *them*. Second of all, white kids won't want me in their old club. So there!"

By this time, Pat was too worked up to sit still. She began to roll her eyes, crossing them and un-crossing them. "Please take me in your club," she said in a high piping voice. "See the way I can roll my eyes. And you ought to see me dance!" Pat pretended to do the twist. She wiggled as if she didn't know which part of her anatomy should go up and which part should go down. She pretended to get stuck. "Help me . . . oh, oh, I'm stuck. . . ." she cried.

Just then. Mrs. Oliver came out drying her hands. "My, you're quite a little actress," she said, smiling. "I wish I had your talent." Mrs. Oliver turned to Jo-Jo, "Ready for your lesson?"

The idea of lessons reminded Pat of school. "I gotta go home now," she said to Mrs. Oliver, and waving good-by to Lucy Mae and Jo-Jo, she ran quickly out of the yard and across the street. She didn't quite understand why she ran. All she knew was she didn't want Mrs. Oliver to find out how stupid she was in reading. And she wanted time to think more about why Lucy Mae was so scared.

That night, while she was thinking about Lucy Mae's worry, Pat overheard her parents discussing the bus passes, and she realized that September was getting awfully close.

The bus tickets would cost a dollar a month. That dollar meant a lot to the family. Her two big brothers in junior high school delivered orders every day and brought money home. For an allowance, they got only fifty cents a month.

Pat was in bed, but her parents' voices carried into the room where she slept. Across the room, in the bunk bed, the twins were sleeping noisily. On the adjacent wall, in the second bunk bed, she heard Junior turn and twist in his sleep. Under her, Carl was snoring gently. Her parents' voices had stopped. Everything was as usual, yet suddenly the room had become strange.

The window blinds began to clatter ominously from the night wind. The traffic light on the corner cast a menacing shadow on the wall. The room seemed to become smaller, more crowded. It was then that her blackness hit Pat with all its force.

Her hand was out. She was staring at it. But she couldn't see it. It was right in front of her. Yet she couldn't see it. If she put her hand out to stop a car at night—no one would see it. At night— she couldn't be seen. If the white kids threw her in some dark closet. . . .

"Carl! Carl!" she cried, and leaped down into the bed below her. "Carl, save me."

Her thirteen-year-old brother woke up with maddening slowness.

"Carl," Pat begged. "Please get up. You've *got* to stop Mama and Papa from sending me to that all white school."

"Go to sleep. They aren't sending you anywhere this time of the night."

"Carl. Look at your hand." Pat dragged his hand from under the sheet. "Look at it."

"What's to see?" Carl said sleepily.

"That's what I'm telling you," Pat whispered. "Now look at this." She held up the white sheet.

Carl sighed. "That's the sheet. What about it?"

"Did you see your hand?" Pat waited. "Did you see my hand?"

"No. Of course not. That's why we have to wear light colors at night. Mama's told us that—all children should."

"Carl, please listen. If I go to school and the

kids shove me in a dark closet and they take off all my clothes, nobody will ever find me." Pat shivered and Carl put his arm around her.

"Gee. Gee whizz," he whispered.

The door opened. "What's wrong?" Mr. Marley asked in a loud whisper. "You, Frank?"

"No, Pa, it's me," Pat whispered back. "Pa, I'm scared. Please don't buy me a bus pass. Please don't send me to that school."

Mr. Marley picked her up in his arms and, big as she was, he carried her to the living room couch which opened into a bed. Mrs. Marley sleepily tucked Pat under the covers with her. Carl came and sat at the edge while Pat cried out her story.

"Why am I black, Mama? Is it like Carl heard from that boy in school? Am I black because I can't learn. If you're black, does it mean you're stupid?"

Her father spoke. "Maybe . . . your ma's smarter than me and she's lighter than me. I never went past third grade."

Mrs. Marley put the light on with a sharp click. She reached for her husband's hand. "Sam, don't you say that to the children. I went to school up North. You went in the South. What kind of school did you have down there? And what's more, Sam Marley, you're the best husband and the best father and the smartest man in the whole world."

"That's right," Pat said, and smothered her father in an embrace that pulled him down on the bed.

"And what's more, Patricia Marley, I don't want to hear another word out of you about your looks or about your brains. They are as good as the best."

In five minutes, she had Pat convinced that all she had to do was "believe in herself and be good."

"I can be good," Pat told her, "but nobody sees much use in that."

"You be good. They'll see good in it. Just remember, white folks come in all colors and Negroes come in all colors and shades. But one is as good as the other. And don't you forget it. Maybe you'll grow up to be a big star actress, or a school teacher like Mr. Oliver. Maybe Carl and Junior will go to high school and get to be mechanics." Her mother's voice grew dreamy. "If you work hard in the school across town, then the twins will go when they get to be in fifth grade . . . and Ginny." Her mother smiled at the thought of Ginny, now in first grade, ever getting to be as big as Pat. She tweaked Pat's nose and added, "Just do what you know is right and do it the best you can."

Pat nuzzled close to her mother and held tight to her father's hand. Her toes curled snugly against Carl. Before long, her mother had convinced her that white children would treat her the way she treated them.

"You listen like the white kids do, and you'll be as smart as the smartest. Mind me. Don't know where we're going to get a dollar every month for your bus pass and your lunch, but we're going to get it. Go to sleep now . . . hurry . . . your ma and pa got to do some extra work so you can have a new dress and shoes."

Pat was tucked into bed and fell asleep almost at once. She saw herself riding in a big bus with Jo-Jo at her side. Beside them sat dozens of brown-skinned boys and girls. Some even as dark as Pat. Down the avenue that bus went until it reached a school made all of white marble. There her dream stopped and she fell into dreamless sleep.

chapter 3

The next morning, Pat awoke to Ginny's squeals. "Get up. We're *all* going shopping. We're going to get school things!"

"For real?" Pat bounced out of bed. "Ma, are we? Are you going to buy a dress for me like the one Lucy Mae wore in assembly? Are you? And *is* Papa coming?"

"He's going to tend to the hot water now. Carl will wipe down the front hall at three o'clock when he comes from the store."

"Whee—ee." Pat danced into the bathroom. She had only been to the big shopping center once. Bus fare for the family was high, and Mrs. Marley thought the money could be used for some extra dessert instead of giving it to the bus company.

When the twins and Ginny were dressed and waiting at the door, and Pat was buckling her sandals, and Mrs. Marley had twice changed her mind about how much money she was going to take out of the teapot, Frank insisted on finding out what was keeping his father.

"Go ahead," Mrs. Marley said hesitantly, "but keep clean. Mind you don't get dirty."

"Tell Pa to hurry," Pat said. "Maybe somebody else will buy the dress I want."

"Pat, you can't count on finding exactly Lucy Mae's dress," Mrs. Marley said as she took an extra dollar out of the teapot, then set it back on the shelf.

Pat knew her mother was right but continued the argument. She wanted to talk and think about the kind of dress she was going to buy. "Well, I want one with a big collar. If we are going to school together, I don't want to look like her slave."

"Patricia Marley, where do you get such ideas? Mr. Oliver is a school teacher and your father is a handy man. You've got so stop thinking about clothes all the time."

"Yeah," Willy said with conviction. "Just because you're going across town to school, you think you're special. Big deal!"

"And you'd better mind your tongue, William

Marley. It *is* a big deal. Your papa is going to work two jobs so Pat can look nice."

Mrs. Marley turned toward the door, saw no sign of her husband, then turned to the bureau in the living room. Under her husband's shirts, she found a square paper parcel. "You know how your pa hates to go buying things for girls? Well, last week he bought this. For Pat. Because he wants her not to be ashamed."

Pat leaped to corral the present. "No," her mother said. "He wants to give it to you himself. Where is that man?"

That was when they heard Frank's feet pounding up the stairs. There was an urgency in the regular pattern of noise his shoes made on the wooden treads.

Pat was at the door first. Her mother seemed frozen near the kitchen table. Pat didn't talk. She didn't need to. As soon as Frank saw her, he emitted a strange, unnerving cry.

"E—eee—ee."

Pat dug her fingers into Frank's arm. "What are you screaming for?"

Frank ran past her and threw his arms around his mother. "Papa," he cried.

Mrs. Marley put her arms around Frank. She tried to form a word, but her lips didn't move. Willy and Ginny stood wide-eyed.

"Talk!" Pat demanded. "Where's Papa?"

"Downstairs. Mama, Papa's dead."

"Liar!"

Pat's denial rang throughout the building as she flew down the stairs. When she got down to the basement, she found Mr. Meadows near her father.

"I came to bring the old newspapers down," Jo-Jo's father said. "I think your father fell. Go get your ma."

Mrs. Marley was already coming down the stairs. "Sam! Sam!" she was calling.

Pat stood aside, holding back the twins and Ginny. Jo-Jo's father and her mother were on their knees. Mr. Meadows was going over her father's body gently, and her mother was moaning. Not knowing how else to help, Pat ran to the sink and brought a cup of water.

When at last Mr. Marley opened his eyes and took a sip of the water, Pat shut her own eyes, overwhelmed with gratitude that her father was not dead.

"I was reaching for the light switch. Must have slipped," her father murmured.

Mrs. Marley was breathing heavily. "Thank God. Thank God. Want any help up?"

But Mr. Marley couldn't get up. "Something the matter with my legs," he said, his lips ashen.

Then Pat noticed how queerly his legs were arranged. One going out at an angle from his left side and the other folded under his body.

"Maybe his leg is broken," she cried, a picture forming of Cindy Warren's broken leg and the cast she had worn for over a month. "Call an ambulance," Pat said with authority.

"Smart girl. Your Pat is a smart girl," Mr. Meadows said. "I'll run over to the drugstore and call the hospital."

"Mrs. Andrews got a telephone," Frank suggested helpfully. But the grownups thought the drugstore was quicker and Pat went with Mr. Meadows, just in case the druggist had any idea of what to do until the doctor came.

The next hour or two remained a blur for Pat. There was the terror and the waiting. There was the sight of her father carried up the cellar stairs on a stretcher.

"Give Pat her present," was the last thing her father said to Mrs. Marley before the doctor closed the ambulance door.

Mrs. Marley was sitting next to her husband in the ambulance. She called out, as the door shut, "Mind the children, Pat. Tell Carl and Junior to come to Elmhurst Hospital. Tell them to hurry."

The crowd that had gathered thinned out. Mr.

Meadows wanted the Marleys to come to his house. The twins wanted to go to the store and get Carl and Junior.

"Maybe they'd better go," Pat said, glad to find a way to refuse Mr. Meadows gracefully. She wanted to be alone to think about what had happened. She thought about the trip to the shopping center. Maybe if her father hadn't been in a hurry to buy her new clothes, he might not have slipped. It was because of her selfishness that he was now lying in pain on a hospital stretcher.

Carl and Junior went directly to the hospital without changing their clothes. When the twins came back, Pat had her hands full trying to calm them down. They wanted to go to the hospital, too.

"We can't go," Pat explained. "Only over thirteen can you visit the hospital."

It made her feel better to explain to the younger ones something she had been told; she didn't fully understand the reason herself. When her mother returned, she intended to question that ruling.

She put on the rice at five o'clock. Then she remembered that Papa was supposed to wash down the front hall Saturday afternoons when the regular man was off. Carl couldn't do it, he had gone to be with her mother at the hospital.

Heavy as the mop was, Pat pushed it across the floor energetically. It had taken the three of them—Pat and the twins, Willy and Frank—to carry the pail full of water up from the basement. But Pat, alone, managed to wring out the mop and clean the linoleum. The work made the time pass faster.

When at last Mrs. Marley and the older boys returned from the hospital, Pat ran to her mother's arms fearfully.

"Papa is going to be all right, Pat," Mrs. Marley said.

Pat wanted to speak, to tell how it had been her fault, but before she could say anything, her mother went on. "Pat, you're a brave girl to have stayed here and looked after the children."

Pat beamed.

"Pat washed the hall, too," said Ginny. "And I helped!"

Pat hugged her little sister and modestly made little of the job.

Mrs. Marley smiled at all her children. "Now, Papa's got a broken hip and he's worried about his work here. We've all got to do something to hold on to his job until his hip heals."

The children listened big-eyed while Mrs. Marley told them about their father. He had been X-rayed.

The doctor had said an operation was best and Mrs. Marley had agreed that somehow money would be found for it. "Papa's hip is broken in two places. This operation is better than a cast. In a month, he'll be home. And the doctor is going to let us pay little by little."

Junior asked, "How come my friend's father didn't have to pay when he was in the hospital?"

Pat looked at him coldly. How could he worry about money at such a time?

Mrs. Marley's eyes filled with tears. "Maybe your friend's family was a welfare case. If we went begging, maybe. . . ." She put her arm around Pat. "We may be poor but we'll work and pay our own way."

"You can take the money from the teapot," Willy said.

"I don't really need a dress," Pat added.

"And I can wear my sneakers to school," Frank said.

"Your papa will be proud of you. But your clothes money is only a tiny bit."

Pat saw a tiny pulse near her mother's mouth begin beating and, with a surge of emotion she didn't recognize, Pat threw her arms around her mother and hugged furiously.

The next day didn't seem much like a Sunday. Carl and Junior went down into the basement to do the chores for the building. All morning, Mrs. Marley darned and hemmed to make up for the lost Saturday, and a long line of clothes was drying on the roof, ready for ironing. No one said a word about new things for school.

While Mrs. Marley pinned a hem on one of the dresses which Pat had outgrown, Pat thought of the dress she might have had. But it was the thought of the money to be spent on lunch and bus fares which made her say, "Maybe I ought to stay in P.S. 27!"

Her mother's eyes met hers coldly. "No more of that talk. Your pa wouldn't rest if he thought that you weren't going to the new school on account of his accident. We'll get the money. And your pa bought you that present especially for the new school."

It was then, for the first time, that Pat remembered the square package. In all her life, she had never before forgotten to open a present. Where had she put it?

She finally found it under the jeans that needed patches. "What did Papa get me?" she asked as she feverishly pulled off the wrappings. "A pocketbook!" she cried out joyfully. "Just like the ones the high school girls have!"

Mrs. Marley smiled sadly. "He wanted you to have one, too. That's how he is—always thinking of others."

To keep from crying, Pat became busy, too. She showed Ginny how to write the letter G. She helped her mother serve a quick lunch before going off to the hospital.

Jo-Jo and his mother came up after Mrs. Marley had gone.

"We met Lucy Mae in the shopping center when we went yesterday, and I got new shoes and a new suit and she. . . ."

"Jo-Jo, where's your common sense?" Mrs. Meadows asked. "Here's Patricia worried about her pa, and you're jabbering about clothes."

Pat acted as grownup as could be. She refused to meet Jo-Jo's eyes and she thanked Mrs. Meadows for coming up. "And thank you for inviting us to supper," she said, "but my mother has supper cooking." Then she added, "I'm watching it carefully."

"As long as you're getting on all right," said Mrs. Meadows.

"See you tomorrow," Jo-Jo said as his mother dragged him after her out of the apartment.

"See you—" Pat echoed, but her heart wasn't in

it. The story of Jo-Jo's shopping expedition hurt despite her determination not to think of clothes. She had wanted so much to look nice.

Later, Mrs. Oliver came up and asked what she could do to help.

Pat told her politely the same thing she had said to Mrs. Meadows. "My mother has taken care of everything."

"Do you want Lucy Mae to call for you tomorrow?" Mrs. Oliver asked.

Pat thought fast. Here was Mrs. Oliver dressed in a blue-and-white cotton suit such as Pat saw in advertisements. In the kitchen, Mrs. Oliver, in her high-heeled shoes and polished fingernails, looked out of place. Pat didn't feel comfortable with Mrs. Oliver. Mrs. Oliver spoke in a "teacher" voice. Her words came out clipped, each "d" and "t" were heard. Lucy Mae talked that way, too. Pat thought about the long trip across town with Lucy Mae. What would they talk about?

"No, thank you. I don't know what time I'm going tomorrow," Pat answered, telling only part of the truth.

She was glad when Mrs. Oliver left.

At dinner, when she told her mother about their visitors and the offers of help, she didn't mention her refusal to ride with Lucy Mae. And the next morning, Pat helped Ginny get dressed, then hurried through her breakfast while her mother was down in the basement.

At seven-forty-five, her mother came up, tied a dollar and a quarter into a handkerchief, and gave it to Pat. "Put the money and your lunch into your pocketbook. When the teacher collects the dollar and gives you your pass, put that in your pocketbook. Fifteen cents is for bus fare this morning. You'll have ten cents change. You'll have the bus pass for the trip home. But don't lose the pass—or the dime! Watch for the avenue I've got written on the paper. Maybe Mrs. Oliver will go with you."

Pat said yes to everything, threw a kiss, and ran down to Jo-Jo's.

"I'm going with Lucy Mae," Jo-Jo said brightly. "Aren't you? I thought you were going with. . . ."

Pat didn't even let him finish his sentence. Her feelings were too hurt. She forgot that she had refused Mrs. Oliver's offer. All she could think of was that Jo-Jo, her special friend, was going with Lucy Mae.

"So, go ahead. Who's stopping you?" Pat flung at him and dashed madly out of the building, almost knocking over two people coming in. It was at the corner that she realized the two people were Lucy Mae and Mrs. Oliver.

"I don't care," Pat told herself untruthfully as she joined the group of people getting on the bus. "I don't need anybody. Especially big-mouth Jo-Jo Meadows."

The door of the bus closed and, with a fluttering heart, Pat began her first trip across town.

chapter 4

Pat was no sooner in the bus, her fifteen cents in the coin box, than she regretted running away from Jo-Jo. Now she wished he were near. Even Lucy Mae, in a new dress and new shoes, would be welcome. The big bus was filled with people who seemed set on shoving her away from the only handhold she had been able to grasp.

She was hanging on to the back of a seat. On both sides, there were boys and girls taller than she. It was impossible to read the map she clutched.

"Move back in the bus!" the driver shouted at each stop. "Everybody step back."

"Concord Avenue. I have to go to Concord Avenue," Pat mumbled, hoping that the boy on her right might hear her and tell her what to do. But the boy was talking to a girl on her left and didn't hear. A woman behind her heard, and Pat felt a hand on her shoulder.

"I'll tell you when we get there," the woman said. "I get off after you."

Pat wiggled around until she could see the woman. The woman's brown face looked sad. "That's a long way to go to school for such a little girl!" she said, and Pat felt comforted at once.

The woman swung around to Pat's side and, somehow, Pat found herself with enough room to stand straight. It was good to have both arms where she could use them and no need to watch each street corner. She knew the woman would tell her when to get off.

"Next one," said the woman, after what seemed like hours of riding time. "Lots of luck!" And, with a wedgelike movement of her arm, she cleared the way for Pat to get to the door.

"Thanks," Pat called as she stepped into the street. And the woman smiled, pointing toward the east, her mouth forming the words, "That way."

No other children got off the bus, but there were many children on the street. Pat saw at a glance that they were white and knew each other. They met and began talking loudly about their vacations as they started in the direction of the school. Pat had never felt so alone, so desolate.

The unfamiliar street of tall apartment houses, some with canopies and one with a doorman, frightened her. Cold and quiet, they seemed to stare back at her with a warning. Every window was closed and blank. No blind was open and, all along the street, she heard a strange whirring sound which, she discovered later, belonged to air conditioning units.

Although she wore a sweater and the sun was shining, Pat was chilled. She walked faster and faster, and swung her new pocketbook on her finger. She passed children walking in pairs, but no one noticed her. They were all white faces. Only the thought of her father lying sick in the hospital kept Pat from turning around and running home.

"I'll do it if it kills me!" she promised herself. "My daddy wants me to come, and I'm going to do it!"

But, when she reached the school and saw the big schoolyard bordered by yellow and pale violet flowers, with benches set in a circle in the center, and a sandbox and a jungle gym, she stopped short. There were dozens of girls and boys—all white— standing inside the gate, and all talking. There were six doors. Which one should she use? Did

she dare take out the post card with her name and class? Could she ask someone? If only Jo-Jo and Lucy Mae were with her. . . .

She sidled up to a group of girls about her age. One of the girls, with reddish hair and pale lemon-colored skin, was taller than the others, taller even than Pat, and her thin arms and legs were never at rest. She was hopping, dodging, pumping, and looking around as she talked. Talk! Talk! Talk! That was what she seemed to do without stopping.

Pat tried to go around the group from one side and then the other. The girls were all listening intently to the tall girl's story. It was about a camping trip and a leaky canoe. At frequent intervals, the girls "oohed" and begged for more details which the tall girl gladly supplied. Pat found herself eavesdropping, although the story didn't seem interesting to her. This girl had no sense if she took a leaky canoe and went out onto the lake just for kicks!

"Gee, you're always causing a riot!" a brown-haired girl called out amid general laughter.

Another one howled. "Just like in class after assembly last June. Remember? When Sarah put black finger paint on her face, and made believe she was one of the Negro children coming into school this year!"

A pit of agony opened in Pat's chest as the girl

in the center widened her lips with her fingers and, in broad dialect, cried out, "Yas—sah, Principal Mr. Lew-is. I gon-na bring you broth-a-hood!"

The other girls doubled up with laughter and Pat grimly set her teeth. With both hands locked on her drawstring bag, she side-stepped the group and blindly stamped her way to an open door.

"Hello!"

The warm welcome made Pat raise her eyes. She lowered them quickly. In front of her stood a middle-sized woman with middling brown hair and glasses. A teacher. Pat had seen hundreds like her.

"Hello! I'm Mrs. Klein. Can I help you?"

Pat yanked her identification card out of her pocketbook. Her eyes went back toward the yard where the tall girl could be seen still pretending to be a Negro.

The teacher saw Pat's movement. She took Pat's card and, before looking at it, said lightly, "That's Sarah Mellon, the school comedy star. She loves to act."

Pat wanted to say, "She doesn't have to make fun of us," but didn't.

The teacher was examining the card carefully. "Patricia Marley. You're in my class. And Sarah is, too. If I remember rightly, you're also interested in dramatics."

And, before Pat could move, she heard Mrs. Klein call out into the yard, "Sarah! Sarah, come and meet your buddy!"

Pat watched the lanky girl disentangle herself from the other girls. Her hair went flying upward as she scrambled for the things she had dropped in her hurry. Her pencil case, handkerchief, and comb were collected from the grass, from the bushes, and from under the bench before she came loping toward the open door.

Mrs. Klein laughed out loud. "That Sarah!"

Pat drew back into the shadow of the stairwell. "This white teacher is for the birds," she thought, and added, "and that Sarah isn't going to be any buddy of mine. She's as funny as a crutch."

Sarah was finishing a story as she ran and it was Phyllis, the brown-haired girl, who spoke to Mrs. Klein first. "Gee, Sarah has us in stitches. She's acting out how Mr. Lewis looked when he came into class after assembly and saw her doing the twist. You know—before our teacher came in. She had her face all painted black like a. . . ."

Phyllis met Pat's eyes and lowered hers at once. Pat couldn't hide the hatred which was flooding through her body. These white girls had no right to make fun of Negroes. The Negroes had been invited to come to this school. Sarah had better watch out. That was all Pat dared think, but she found her fingers balling into fists.

Mrs. Klein explained to Pat, "Sarah was severely punished for that trick. Weren't you, Sarah?"

Sarah hooted. "They put me into the 5-6 class instead of into 5-1, like my mother wanted. They thought they were punishing me." Sarah explained to Pat. "Ha! Last year's teacher didn't like my acting, but Mrs. Klein lo-ves actresses. And I'm going to lo-ve 5-6 because Mrs. Klein puts on the best plays, and because you are always laughing," she finished, pointing to Mrs. Klein.

Pat kept as far from the group as she dared. Teachers and pupils weren't this chummy where she came from. She watched and listened.

Mrs. Klein's voice grew sharp momentarily. "But Sarah, I will not have you play-acting at the wrong times. Plays are prepared and then presented. Good actors always rehearse and rehearse."

Sarah nodded. Her face looked funny when she was serious. Pat almost pitied the girl for her long nose which became longer when her mouth was shut.

"Now Sarah, off you go to the yard to show Patricia where we line up. Phyllis, you go, too. And mind you, no whispering in the hall."

As Pat turned to walk behind the girls, Mrs. Klein put out her hand formally. "I hope you will like us and be as happy here as we are to have you.

I'm sure Sarah will find a way to tell you everything you need to know before you get to the main hall. Good luck!" She dismissed the girls with a smile so winning that Pat almost forgot to be suspicious of her motives. She found the corners of her own mouth turning up.

"She's the greatest," Sarah said as soon as they had left the stairwell. "Wow! I like being in Mrs. Klein's class. It's a ball. Say, I hear you like to play-act, too. How about you and me making up a puppet show or. . . ."

They had come into the main corridor and Phyllis tugged on Sarah's arm. "Shh!"

Sarah lowered her voice. "I thought Mr. Lewis was a dope—making me your buddy—when he's always yelling at me, especially after he told me that you liked play-acting. . . ."

Pat swung her bag on her finger. One inch higher and it would have hit Sarah. Instead of falling back, Sarah leaped toward the bag. For a second, Pat thought Sarah was after the pocketbook, and she stopped the swing and held tight with both hands.

"Say, that's a swell bag," Sarah said. "Gosh, I always wanted one like that. How did you get such a good bag? Where did you get it?"

"I didn't steal it!" Pat said from between her teeth.

Sarah opened her eyes and her mouth and let

loose a shriek of joy. "Listen to that! You're my speed. A comeback every time."

Pat didn't know what to make of that laugh. She looked through her lashes at Phyllis, who was looking at her. Phyllis was half-smiling. Pat scowled. She was determined not to be taken in by this loud-mouthed girl. Poodle-face wasn't going to make a monkey out of Pat. No—sir—ee. She held back her anger and kept her fists tightened on her pocketbook.

Sarah reached over and grabbed Pat's hands. Her white arms next to Pat's dark ones frightened Pat.

"Look!" said Sarah with that crazy smile. "Isn't this a perfect black-and-white soda?" She nudged Phyllis, who was holding her face rigidly serious. "Which do you prefer—chocolate or vanilla?"

Pat bit hard on her lips. She wanted to cry or hit or run away. If only Jo-Jo would come. She needed him. She needed someone of her own. This white school was no place for her. She was lonely. Scared and awfully, awfully lonely.

chapter 5

Jo-Jo and Lucy Mae came into the indoor yard with a large group of Negro children. They had had to wait a long time for a bus to pick them up. All the buses had been too full to take them on. As they came in, Mr. Lewis, the principal, was making a welcome-back speech to all the classes.

"And a special welcome to our new friends," he boomed out, looking at Pat. She wanted nothing more than a place to sink into.

"Here he goes again," someone whispered in her ear.

Pat looked from the corner of her eye and saw by Sarah's exaggerated woebegone expression that it had been she. There wasn't time to react because it was then that Jo-Jo's group came all the way into the yard.

"What happened to you?" Mr. Lewis asked with a smile.

From the center of the group a girl was thrust forward. It was Lucy Mae looking, Pat thought, like a fairy princess dressed in a filmy blue dress with a million pleats.

"We're sorry, Mr. Lewis. Four buses passed us by. From now on we shall have to get to the bus stop before the crowd."

Pat watched Jo-Jo. He was sucking on his lips; he did that all the time when he was nervous.

Mr. Lewis rubbed his palms together. "Well, we'll have to take care of that. Now, don't you worry. Everything will be taken care of." He beamed at each child, but Pat was glad she wasn't in that group.

"Like a crocodile. . . ." Sarah whispered, and Pat couldn't help but agree. That was pretty much what she had been thinking. How had the white girl guessed? Pat sniffed. Sarah could take it as a laugh or any other way she chose.

The brown-haired girl in front of Pat sniffed, too. She leaned back, and said to Pat without turning around, "Better watch out. Blabbermouth Sarah will get you into trouble. She gets everyone into trouble!"

Pat was surprised. Girls shouldn't go tattling. Especially to strangers—and Pat was a complete stranger.

While the whispering had been going on, Jo-Jo had been directed to the Class 5-6 line. Pat had forgotten that she had ever been angry with him.

"In here, Jo-Jo," she whispered, and motioned to a place by her left side.

Jo-Jo held his eyes unblinkingly open. It was as if he were walking in a dream, only he was still sucking hard on his lips. He followed the monitor to the end of the boys' line. Pat looked to see what had become of Lucy Mae. She had been led to Class 5-1 and a blonde little girl with curls was making room for her. Everyone was smiling—even Lucy Mae.

Mrs. Klein raised her hand for silence, although no one was talking. "Sarah, you know where to stop, so you and Patricia come up front and lead the line," she said. "Forward!"

The brown-haired girl whispered again, "Just because she's in the dramatic club, she's teacher's pet! Mrs. Klein doesn't care *what* Sarah does as long as she takes part in the stupid plays."

"Say, what's your name?" Pat wanted to change

the subject before Sarah or Mrs. Klein heard.

"Deborah Bondy," the brown-haired girl answered, just as Sarah darted forward, calling, "Are you coming, Patricia? Mrs. Klein is waiting."

Slowly, Pat walked to the front of the line. She didn't like such an exposed position and particularly didn't want to be first on the boys' line. She set herself directly ahead of the first girl.

"You go on the boys' line," she said flatly to Sarah. She meant the poodle-haired girl to know that she, Patricia Marley, was not going to be pushed around.

Sarah shrugged. "Come on. Hurry. I want to see if anything happened to the puppet theater over the summer."

As they turned a corner, Pat leaned toward Sarah.

"What puppet theater?" she asked.

Sarah laughed out loud. "Wait until you see it. It's a wow!"

And it was! Mrs. Klein let Sarah show the puppet theater to Pat and to the other children almost as soon as seats were assigned.

Sarah pulled the tiny curtain, turned a knob, and brought forth a little balcony. She reached into a box and, in a twinkling, changed the scene from living room to lake.

"These are some of the puppets we made in the

club last year," she told Pat, and Pat touched each one reverently.

"Can I make one?" Pat asked.

"I guess so. If you join the club," Sarah said evenly. She started to put the furniture and puppets away.

"Can anyone join your club?" Pat asked, after a pause.

"Not . . . the. . . ." Sarah looked at Pat. "Say, maybe you're *not* a bus child! You came so much earlier than the others. Mrs. Klein said that the bus children could not stay after three because of their passes and the long trip." Her face was alive again and her hands were flying as fast as her tongue.

Again, Pat felt confused. She was sure she ought not to like Sarah, but Sarah acted as if she didn't mind what anyone thought. The tall girl's face was as bright as a birthday candle. She *seemed* to want Pat to be in her club.

"Club is the best part of school. Gee, Patricia, it's super! Say, can I call you Pat? Patricia is too long."

Pat shrugged.

"Girls, enough play with the puppet stage. Back to your seats," said Mrs. Klein.

Pat walked down her aisle as Sarah matched

steps in the next one. They sat next to each other in the third row back. Jo-Jo was two rows behind and across the room, alongside the bulletin boards. The brown-haired girl, Deborah, was across the aisle from Pat in the third row. As Pat slid into her seat, the girl pressed a note into her hand.

REMEMBER WHAT I TOLD YOU.
YOUR FRIEND, DEBBY.

"Can I come back early at lunch time and show Pat how to make a puppet? Mrs. Klein, is Pat a bus child? I hope. . . ."

Mrs. Klein rapped sharply on the desk. "Quiet. In the fifth grade you should know how to raise your hand. This is not the time to talk about puppets."

"But can I?" Sarah called out.

"Enough!"

Pat was sorry that Sarah had brought that tone into Mrs. Klein's voice. To Pat, that tone meant punishment papers, extra homework, hands on head. She looked across at Deborah. The brown-haired girl had "I told you so" written all over her face. Pat was glad to look away and see Sarah's embarrassed grin. At least Sarah didn't say mean things about other people!

The morning was busy. An arithmetic test first. Pat was the last one to hand in her paper. Mrs.

Klein stood behind her.

"Are you counting on your fingers, Patricia?" she said softly, so as not to embarrass Pat.

"No. No, I'm not," Pat lied. She hoped that Sarah hadn't heard Mrs. Klein or seen her counting under her desk. Pat couldn't face having the children laugh at her.

"Fifth graders should know all their number facts—addition, subtraction, and multiplication," Mrs. Klein said.

Pat nodded miserably. She knew how to do the examples, but it took forever to do them. It seemed that each time her class was about to learn a new times table, Pat had been sent to the principal's office for acting up. By the time she returned, the class would be on a different table—or so it seemed to Pat. Soon, all the tables had gotten jumbled and it was useless to try to sort them out. And now, this move to a new school had thoroughly confused her. *All* their number facts? Pat wasn't sure she could *ever* learn them all!

Then came a spelling test. Words she had never heard before were given. There had been a few at the beginning that Pat could spell easily, but soon she couldn't spell any of the words Mrs. Klein said. While Sarah and Deborah wrote on, Pat sought Jo-Jo's eyes. He looked as miserable as she felt. But there was no time for feeling sorry.

A monitor came into the classroom to arrange for the bus passes. Pat and Jo-Jo, after the spelling test, went to the principal's office and came out with freshly-typed cards which had name, address, and school number. Pat now felt quite grown-up. The staircase back to her classroom was not as unfamiliar as it had been the first time up. The white monitors not quite as strange as they had been.

Pat felt buoyant and tried to explain what she was thinking to Jo-Jo. "Since we don't go on the regular school bus but on city buses, we *could* stay after school. Then I could join the dramatic club. I'll make a puppet!"

Jo-Jo nodded. "Yeah. Say, did you see my new wallet? My father bought it. Isn't it great?"

Pat looked at it, but without great interest. She swung her new drawstring bag, but Jo-Jo didn't ask about it. Pat didn't care. Talking about the dramatic club and the puppet theater was better than talking about wallets and purses.

"Which puppet do you like the best?" she asked.

"I don't know. I didn't look at them. Say, are you going to eat lunch with the rest of us?"

Pat wasn't listening. Jo-Jo seemed to be miles away from her. How could he have missed seeing the puppets? Boys! Phooey! She walked ahead towards the classroom, leaving the monitors and Jo-Jo behind.

Pat walked into the room with her head high. Both Deborah and Sarah looked up in greeting. Pat didn't smile at either of them, but she didn't move away when Sarah leaned over to talk to her.

"I put your name on the labels. We got arithmetic and social studies books," Sarah whispered.

Pat suddenly wanted to confide in her. "I got my bus pass," she said. "But I can take any bus home I want. Now I can be in the dramatic club, can't I?"

"That's the black-and-white truth," Sarah said with a laugh and bounced around in her seat.

For some reason, Pat wasn't offended. She felt that Sarah wasn't being nasty, wasn't poking fun at her. She knew, somehow, that Sarah would be delighted to have her in the club.

Mrs. Klein rapped for quiet, but her eyes smiled. "I see Sarah is eager to get to work on her social studies," she said with great seriousness.

"No, I'm not," Sarah called out. "I'm itching to get to work on my puppets!"

Pat saw Deborah watching Sarah closely. Her eyes were definitely unfriendly. Pat had seen many unfriendly eyes and she didn't like them. Not in brown faces and not in white. Not when they looked at her, and not when they looked at some-one else. She moved closer in her seat to Sarah's side and met Sarah's glance. Both girls smiled.

"I like the fat girl puppet best," Pat whispered. "Can I make a play up?"

"Not a word about puppets until half past twelve," Mrs. Klein said firmly. "Anyone who comes up after lunch can begin planning to make a puppet. Until then—open your notebooks."

"I like Mrs. Klein," Pat thought. "She makes us work, but she likes fun, too." Pat took her pencil determinedly and began to write in her notebook.

chapter 6

At lunch time, Pat found more things to like about the school which had, at first, frightened her so. She liked the way tables had been arranged along the side of the indoor yard. From the outside windows, she saw the garden and the children walking home for lunch. Despite the barrenness of the huge ground floor area, Pat felt warmth and color in the room because of the view from the windows.

"Say, Pat," Jo-Jo whispered, as Mrs. Klein led them to the tables where eight children sat together, "look. There are lots of us here. Even more than I came with this morning."

Pat did look. There were at least a dozen tables,

most of them already filled with children. And almost all of them were Negroes—the bus children who lived too far to go home for lunch.

"Here. Sit here," Lucy Mae called softly, and Mrs. Klein walked with them to the table where the light-colored girl sat with several other children who were holding lunch bags. Those lunch bags, Pat knew, were given out by the school to children getting free lunch. Pat had never had to eat a free lunch in school and, to show it, she swung her new pocketbook on her finger. Inside the pocketbook lay her peanut butter and jelly sandwich, made the way she loved it—a little jelly and gobs of peanut butter—and a big red apple. Her mother had wrapped the sandwich in wax paper and had pasted a bit of tape at the ends to keep the sandwich securely closed. Pat hurried to take out her sandwich to show Mrs. Klein she was not a "free-luncher." But Mrs. Klein had disappeared.

"Your teacher looks nice," Lucy Mae said enthusiastically. "Mine is, too. She's tops!"

Pat bit into her sandwich. "We got a puppet stage in our room. You ought to see it. It's big. Big as this—" Pat spread her arms wide to show that two people could stand behind the theater. "I'm going to join the dramatic club and make puppets and. . . ."

"Aw, Pat," Jo-Jo said, "don't go getting excited

about puppets. Anyway, that white dog-faced kid with the mop on her head is the teacher's pet."

"Jo-Jo, you mustn't make fun of the way people look," Lucy Mae reminded him. "We don't like it when people talk about our looks."

"She *does* look like a dog—like a poodle. And she *has* got a mop on her head," Pat declared, wondering why Jo-Jo never talked up for himself.

Instead of rallying to Pat's side, Jo-Jo nodded miserably. "My mother said I should watch my tongue. Gee, why do I always. . . ." His voice trailed off.

Pat resented his cowardice. She had expected him to stick to his guns after her swift defense. She glared at him.

Lucy Mae said soothingly, "I think I know which girl you mean. She was beside Pat in the line. Is that the one?"

"She's my buddy!" Pat declared fiercely, not knowing why she was getting angry at Lucy Mae. "She invited me to join the dramatic club—and everything!" That last was all that Pat could think of. She was far from clear about her feelings toward Sarah Mellon. Or Sarah's for her.

Jo-Jo tossed his empty paper bag in the wastepaper basket a few feet from their table. In disgust, he said, "There she goes! Pat, you shouldn't of stick up for a white girl. You should of. . . ."

"Shouldn't stick up," Lucy Mae said, patiently. "You're not supposed to say 'of'. Say 'have.' And you have to say 'stuck up for.' "

Pat spun around and lifted her brows at Lucy Mae. "Do you always go around teaching everybody?"

Pat was immediately sorry. Lucy Mae's eyes filled with tears. To change the subject, Pat mentioned the puppets. Her mind was filled with games to play with them. It was like being given a whole boxful of new dolls—and right in the classroom, too! Talking about the puppets would really make Lucy Mae smile.

"Did I tell you about the puppets? Gee, Lucy Mae, one was wearing a dress almost like the one you wore as the princess in the play, *Aladdin*. Remember?" she said.

Pat was glad to see Lucy Mae's expression brighten. She hated to see drawn faces. Lots of times at home, when her father sat head down, brooding about something he wanted to buy for the children, she would make him laugh. She was thinking more of him than of Lucy Mae when she began to pretend she was the magician in *Aladdin*.

Pat watched Lucy Mae's face begin to sparkle as, in a voice dripping with insincerity, she wheedled, "If you bring me that dirty old lamp, that measly old, filthy lamp, I'll give you a beautiful baseball."

Jo-Jo sprang to the wastepaper basket and, in a falsetto, cried, "Oh, please throw the ball down to poor unworthy me."

A smile spread over Pat's face. She pretended to think. Then suddenly she swung. Her crumpled empty paper bag went flying over the table and, with a flutter, landed right on Jo-Jo's head.

"Ouch!" he yelled in mock pain.

"Now, give me that lamp, unworthy one," Pat demanded in her magician's voice. She heard the laughter that filled the room.

From somewhere, a huge voice called out, "I'm the genii of the lamp. Command me, master!"

That voice was not Jo-Jo's. Jo-Jo was as surprised as Pat. Every eye was turned now towards the door leading into the indoor yard. Someone was behind the open door. "Rub the lamp and let me out," the voice said.

Pat realized it was Sarah! Sarah had been on her way upstairs. She must have seen the group at the tables and, instead of continuing up the stairs, had joined the play. Pat remembered that Sarah had asked permission to come back early.

As if they had been playing together for years, Pat turned to Sarah and grinned. Then, she put on her magician's face and glared at the wastepaper basket. Jo-Jo had never been good at this type of play-acting. She knew that he would muff the cue, so she tried to keep him quiet.

"Why are you so *quiet* down there?" she asked.

As expected, Jo-Jo didn't know what she wanted. "I want to go out and play," he said in his ordinary voice. "Come on, let's go out and play that game you made up last week. You know, that funny tag."

Sarah roared over Jo-Jo's words, "Let me out, master, and I'll make this dumbbell vanish!"

Now Pat was angry. Game or no game, no one was going to make fun of Jo-Jo. She was about to spring off the bench, but a hand held her back.

"Sarah is still play-acting," Lucy Mae said, and Pat sat down with a thump.

With her hair tangled and slightly moist, as if she had been running too fast, Sarah stalked into the yard.

"Come on," she coaxed. "Let's finish it."

"Yes," said Mrs. Klein, who apparently had been watching from another doorway. "Let's go upstairs and give our puppets a workout. They've been lonely all summer."

"Aw, Pat," Jo-Jo wailed.

"You can come up, too," Mrs. Klein said to him.

Jo-Jo looked at the boys running outside. Then he looked at Pat, who was looking at Sarah dancing on one foot. He got up to join the boys.

"Come on, Pat," urged Sarah. "Before the other kids come. Hurry."

She put out her hand to take Pat's and Pat almost put hers into it. But the sight of the light skin coming towards her made her drop her arm. Her brother Carl had told her once that a white boy thought colored skin was like paint and came off. What if, after she touched Sarah's hand, Sarah began to examine the hand to see if any color had rubbed off. That would be like Sarah. Sarah liked to joke. But certain things shouldn't be joked about. She dropped her hand but her face retained its smile.

"Let's go," she agreed, forgetting about Jo-Jo and about Lucy Mae, who was still sitting at the table. Everyone else had gone.

"Do you like to act?" Mrs. Klein asked Lucy Mae politely.

"I do," Lucy Mae answered, and Pat, from the fullness of her excitement, called back, "Lucy Mae was the star in all her class plays."

"Then, I hope you will join our dramatic group," Mrs. Klein said warmly. "We meet Friday afternoons. I'll get the applications out this afternoon." She smiled and followed Pat out of the yard.

Pat was waiting in the stairwell with Sarah who was telling her how much fun making puppets could be. She was eager to go up to the classroom. She saw Mrs. Klein leave, and the hopeful look on Lucy Mae's face began to fade.

Light skin, or dark skin, Pat recognized misery when she saw it. Lucy Mae was dying to join the group going upstairs. Pretty as she was—Pat guessed —she was feeling much as Pat did when she wanted something very much and couldn't get it.

Suddenly, Pat called out. "Mrs. Klein, can my friend, Lucy Mae, come, too—even if she isn't in our class?"

"Why, of course she can," Mrs. Klein said, after a brief pause.

The look in Lucy Mae's eyes as she walked towards the stairwell made Pat float on clouds of glory. Her mother always told the children, "The best thing to do is the kind thing!" and Pat sent out her wordless thanks for the advice.

"Perhaps Lucy Mae *could* be my friend. And, she does like plays," Pat told herself as the three girls followed Mrs. Klein into the sunlit classroom.

chapter 7

"Did you get to school all right?" Mrs. Marley asked as Pat ran into the house. "Was the bus crowded? When I go across town to that neighborhood, Tuesdays and Fridays, the bus is packed."

With her dress already half off, Pat told her mother that Jo-Jo and Lucy Mae had been caught in the rush. "They came late. I'm glad I didn't go with them," she said, ignoring a twinge of conscience. "You never said the streets were so nice and the houses had doormen and that there were millions of white kids."

Mrs. Marley made a wry face and reached for her long spoon. "What's to tell? I go. I come. Someday, one of my kids is going to live in a house like that. Maybe you." She took the heavy cover off the stew pot and stirred.

Pat sniffed deeply. "Mmmm. When will supper be ready? Gee, Mom, you ought to see the puppet theater in my room."

"Who got puppets?" Ginny demanded from the corner of the kitchen where she was playing. "I want puppets."

While Pat and Mrs. Marley explained, they heard the twins on the stairs.

The boys were yelling, "Carl and Junior say come down to the basement, Ma. Come on down."

That was the end of quiet talk. The hot-water boiler had broken down while Junior was fixing the fire. Now both boys stood beside the furnace with a question on their faces. If they could not fix the furnace, what would the landlord do?

They asked Mrs. Marley right off, "If we got to get a plumber, who'll pay?"

"We will," Mrs. Marley answered promptly. "It's your father's job to keep things repaired. If the landlord has to pay out money, maybe he'll get a new man."

"We know," Junior said, and Carl sighed. "But where are we going to get the money?"

"Don't cross bridges yet," Mrs. Marley answered, and opened the big furnace door. She opened and shut a few more doors, and the boys realized that she was as ignorant of the furnace as they were. Finally, she slammed the big door shut. "Carl. And you, Junior. You're going to go and see your pa in the hospital tonight. You take a pencil and paper. Your pa will tell you what to do."

All the faces brightened. Their father would know how to fix the furnace.

"But didn't he get that pin put in his hip today? Is he going to be able to sit up?" asked Carl.

"He'll be able to talk—and that's all you need. I saw him at two o'clock. He talked then. Just say *furnace* and he'll wake up. Don't you worry."

"But. . . ." It was Junior who was worried now. "What if the tenants start screaming about no hot water?"

Pat, running down the stairs with Ginny, heard the question. "Just tell them to keep quiet," she said. "Don't they know that Papa is in the hospital?"

Mrs. Marley turned around. "What makes you so hot under the collar all the time? Why didn't you stay upstairs with Ginny?"

"I wanted to know what the boys had called you about," Pat answered. "Why do I always have to be left out of everything?"

"Well, I'll give you something to do, so you won't be missing anything," Mrs. Marley answered. "You and the twins go around to the tenants and explain about the hot water. And mind you, be polite. Sweet as pie. Say 'Excuse me' and 'Please' and ask them to be patient. Now, go on! We'll all be put out on the street if the landlord gets himself a new hired man."

That was a job Pat didn't like. She hated asking favors, and this was a big favor. Even when Mr. Marley was home, people would bang on the pipes and come running when the hot water was cut off, even for a short while. The taste of her errand was bitter in her mouth, but she went. She knew that if the tenants called up the landlord and complained about the lack of hot water, the family would suffer.

The twins, tired from running up and down the stairs with Pat, went to bed early and just missed seeing the older boys come back from the hospital. Mrs. Marley asked about Mr. Marley's health and then about the boiler.

"He says to call the plumber this time. If I watch, the next time something goes haywire, I'll be able to fix it," said Junior.

"Then run down the street now. Maybe the plumber on the corner is still in his store. Hurry!" Mrs. Marley urged as she squeezed suds through Pat's soiled school dress.

Junior was going out the door when Mrs. Meadows came in. First, she reassured Mrs. Marley.

"The tenants aren't going to call the landlord. They like your Sam too much to do that!" Then, she asked if the Marleys needed more money. "I got two jobs going begging, if you want a couple of more days' work," she ended.

"We could use the money," Mrs. Marley said, scrubbing the sleeve cuffs.

Carl called in from the living room where he was doing homework on the couch. "Junior and me can scrub down the halls and collect the garbage cans when we come home from school."

Mrs. Meadows sat down at the kitchen table. "You got good kids."

Pat's lip trembled. Always, it seemed to her, the older boys got the compliments because they were bigger and able to do things she couldn't. "You can go to work, Ma," she cried impulsively. "I'll come right home from school and take care of the kids and give them a snack and everything."

Mrs. Marley nodded. "That would be nice, Pat. But I don't like to leave the little ones when you're in one of your black moods."

Pat jumped up from the table where she had been trying to study her four times table. "See! No matter what I do, you blame me. I was real good *today*. No matter what anyone said, I didn't blow my top. Ask anyone!"

Carl popped his head in the kitchen. "If anyone

talks fresh to you, or touches you, you tell me, and I'll. . . ."

Mrs. Marley dropped Pat's dress in the washtub and stared Carl in the eye. "And you'll what?"

"Nothing," Carl said, and dropped his eyes to his notebook, as if in a hurry to get back to it.

Mrs. Marley said nothing for a moment, and then Junior came in to talk about the plumber and the boiler. Pat took her arithmetic book into the living room and sat next to Carl.

"What happened today?" he asked softly.

"Nothing. Just that I can't understand my buddy. First she makes fun of me 'cause I'm black, and then she invites me to make a puppet with her." Pat told him about the dramatic club and Mrs. Klein. "She gave out applications. Mama can sign mine. Right now. Before I forget."

"Hey," Carl said, "how are you going to join any clubs if Mama goes to work every day?"

That stopped Pat cold. What Carl said was true. Who would take care of Ginny and the twins with Papa in the hospital? Yet, she never wanted anything as much as she wanted to be in Mrs. Klein's club. There was but one solution. She walked slowly into the kitchen where Mrs. Meadows was saying good-by.

In her best company manners and brightest smile, Pat said good-by, and then added, "Tell Jo-Jo that tomorrow I'll call for him. Early. So we don't get caught in the rush." She hoped that Mrs. Meadows would stop for a moment longer and talk about the terrible bus situation.

She was right. While they talked, Pat opened her drawstring bag and pulled out her dramatic club application. Mrs. Meadows never failed to stick up for a child. She, like Mrs. Marley, felt children "came first."

Pat opened her application. "Mama," she said, interrupting them, "will you sign this paper for school?"

Before her mother could read it, she said, "It's for a dramatic club. Lucy Mae and me were invited to join. On Fridays." Then she put her hand over her mouth. "Oh," she wailed pathetically, "I can't join. You will be working on Fridays."

Pat watched Mrs. Meadows wink to her mother. Pat read Mrs. Meadows' lips: *Let her. I'll take care of the little ones.*

Mrs. Marley shook her head emphatically. "What's this? How come only you and Lucy Mae? What about Johnny?"

"Now, Pat," said Mrs. Meadows. "No nonsense. I don't mind tending the kids so you can join a club. But what's come between you and Johnny? You ran off to school without him and now you and

Lucy Mae are joining a club without him. Did Johnny do something to you?"

"No, Mrs. Meadows. It's just that Jo-Jo doesn't like plays and puppets. The teacher invited him, but Jo-Jo wants to play outdoors with the boys. And thank you for offering. And, if Jo-Jo wants to join, my buddy, Sarah Mellon, says that the club needs boys, and. . . ."

"What was that name? Sarah Mellon?" Mrs. Meadows asked.

Pat nodded.

"Is she a redheaded, lanky girl that can't stand still and never shuts up?"

Pat nodded. The description, unflattering as it was, certainly fit her buddy.

Mrs. Meadows went on. "It's Mrs. Mellon who needs somebody to take my place. And take my word for it, that Sarah is a real terror. A four-alarm fire. I worked for the family until I got the job in the supermarket. In the two months I worked in that house, I heard enough!"

Mrs. Marley looked at Pat. "How come you got such a terror for a buddy?"

"Teacher picked her for me. Honest, Ma. Ask Lucy Mae."

"I'm asking *you*."

"I'm telling you, Ma." Pat looked straight into

her mother's eyes. She wasn't acting now.

"And what's all this about acting and puppets, with your father in the hospital and just operated on?"

"She's only a child," Mrs. Meadows murmured.

"Ma, only on Fridays. The rest of the week, I'll come home and do like I said." Pat threw her arms around her mother and held tight. Her conscience was fully awake now, but she still wanted to join the dramatic club. It was as if she had caught fire inside and nothing was able to put it out.

Mrs. Marley bent her head low until it touched Pat's. "Honey. You got to learn. Your pa and I want you to go to a good school. A dollar a month the bus pass is . . . and you know we got no money. That dollar pass is for learning."

Pat knew her mother was holding back tears.

"When your pa comes home in a couple of weeks, he's going to want to see how smart you are in that new school. He knows you can act—real good! What he'll want to see is if you can read better, figure your numbers better."

Pat didn't care who was watching as her tears came chasing down her face. "I'm sorry, Mama. Really. But when Papa comes home, if I'm real smart in school, can I . . . will you let me join the club?"

"Let your papa come home, first, honey. Let that

happen first," Mrs. Marley said with a sigh. Then she turned to Mrs. Meadows with a wry smile. "Children. They got little to worry them. Thank God."

Pat closed her eyes. She wanted to burst out with a cry, "That's not true." But she held on to the words. Grabbing her arithmetic book, she ran into the living room and threw herself down next to Carl.

"I'm going to study till I'm blue in the face," she promised. "And I'm going to pray night and day that Papa comes home in a hurry.

Carl rubbed the top of her head. "For luck, Midnight! Just rubbing for luck!"

And, for the moment, it seemed to Pat that the rub worked. Her head stopped aching and the print stopped dancing. She said, resolutely, "Two times four are eight. Three times four are twelve. Four times four. . . ."

chapter 8

On the third day of school, Pat's almost forgotten nightmare became a reality. Lucy Mae was quizzing Pat and Jo-Jo on the four times table as they walked from the bus to the indoor line.

"You know them!" Lucy Mae exclaimed when Pat answered the last one correctly.

"Lucky for us we are on the bus with you!" Pat said. "You know, I used to think you'd be uppity. But you're not."

Lucy Mae's smile was as broad as Pat's as the three separated for their class lines. Lucy Mae was about to say something to Pat, and her eyes were sparkling, when from Jo-Jo's line came a snort followed by a clear boy's voice chanting: "Apes coming to our line. Watch out!"

Jo-Jo stopped in his tracks.

"Yoo-hoo, ape," someone called.

Giggles echoed through the schoolyard.

"Who said that?" Jo-Jo asked. His lower lip came out.

Pat moved over to his side, her pocketbook poised, ready for action.

Then Lucy Mae was beside her. "Shh!" Lucy Mae whispered. "Shh!"

Pat looked around the yard as if she were dreaming. Although she knew there were other Negro children, all she could see were white faces all around. And she was in the middle of the circle, huddled. Jo-Jo was standing razor-stiff, his eyes burning. Lucy Mae was holding on to him.

"Don't answer back," she begged. "Don't move."

Eyes stared. In the second that followed, Pat went through a century of terror. One move, and then an avalanche. Many times in her dreams, she had almost died in such an avalanche. How many times had she heard her mother warn Junior and Carl, "Don't fight white folks. Don't touch them."

She heard Lucy Mae urging, "Don't listen. Pretend we're talking. Don't look."

Pat saw Lucy Mae smiling a smile so lost and terror-filled that it wrenched Pat out of her stupor.

"Quit it, Jo-Jo," she said under her breath. "Play it cool! There's hundreds of 'em."

She put her arm around Lucy Mae. "Is anybody coming?" She asked under her breath. From the protection of Pat's body, Lucy Mae looked. There was no one coming. Just giggles and laughter—and Pat's hands ached. She wanted to push, hit, feel bone against her clenched fists, but she held tight.

With all the breath stored in her lungs, Pat forced out a bellow of laughter. She clapped Jo-Jo on the back with her purse as if he had said something smart-alecky.

"Ha-ha-hoo-ho-ho," she laughed, and prodded Jo-Jo until he joined her.

Carefully, they scanned the faces and backs, and the dark places. The staring eyes had turned away. No further word was flung at them.

"Should we tell a teacher?" Lucy Mae asked softly.

"I'm no chicken," Jo-Jo answered.

Pat filled her lungs again. "I'm going to my line," she said, without moving her lips.

"Remember," Lucy Mae said, "don't listen to what they say. Pretend you don't hear. Jo-Jo? Pat?"

Jo-Jo and Pat walked with extreme casualness with Lucy Mae to the lines. Then, in unison, they each marched to their own line. There was a small burst of titters.

Under his breath, Jo-Jo said, "Bet it's my *buddy* Eric."

"Don't listen. Play it cool," said Pat with her lips spread in a bright smile.

They separated. Pat was the fourth girl on the line. Jo-Jo was the seventh boy. Eric, Jo-Jo's appointed buddy, was the third boy, and Pat tried to study his back. Had he been the one? Why had Jo-Jo not said anything about him before? Eric had not acted suspiciously—not that Pat had noticed. Or did white kids all act nice and then—pop!

The morning became a blur. Pat listened in class, trying to identify the voice that had spoken so cruelly before school. To her ears, suddenly, all the voices were filled with venom. Anyone might have said it. Her head began to swim, and she forced herself to stop listening. Then she found she was hearing the laughter and giggles and the word *ape* over and over again. There seemed no way for her to shut off the clamor in her head.

"Will you read the next example?"

Pat felt a finger poke into her ribs. "Mrs. Klein's talking to you," Sarah whispered, and poked again.

"Wha-what?" Pat gasped.

"The fourth example," Mrs. Klein said quietly.

"Here," Sarah whispered and pointed. Pat followed the finger. From habit, her tongue began to form around the sentence Sarah was pointing to.

Pat read stammeringly, "From the above ill– ill. . . ."

The class began to laugh. Mrs. Klein supplied the word illustration, but Pat couldn't go on. As her tongue stumbled, she looked back to where Jo-Jo sat. But instead of meeting Jo-Jo's friendly eyes, she met his buddy's. The white boy grinned at her, an ugly, insulting grin.

Pat turned away quickly. As she did, she heard from somewhere a whisper, "Apes can't read." At the same second, from the opposite side of the room, the side where Jo-Jo and Eric sat, a spitball came flying.

Whizz. It slapped Pat on the side of her face and dropped with a plink on the floor. Pat clutched her face, nursing the pain. In the silence, Pat heard nothing but the sound of the falling spitball. She knew about spitballs; she had thrown many and been hit before. Yet there was something in this spitball that she had never known before. Something she didn't want to think about. Didn't want to feel.

Mrs. Klein had been walking around the room. She stopped in front of Eric's desk but addressed the entire class. "Never again in my room will anyone say or do such a thing. In my room, we express

feelings in words *and that only with permission,*"
she said.

But Pat wasn't listening. It didn't matter.

It didn't matter that Deborah was leaning toward
her and whispering sympathetically, "That Eric!
He's one of the worst."

It didn't matter that Sarah put her arm around
Pat and talked excitedly about "getting even" and
much more.

Nothing mattered to Pat but the clock slowly
ticking out the minutes before the bell rang and
she could get out of this room filled with enemies.

"I hate them all. I hate them all," she repeated
to herself over and over until, at last, the bell rang.

"Will you stay for a moment?" Mrs. Klein asked.

"Can't," Pat mumbled, hoping that no one was
watching. She didn't dare to say another word, lest
her eyes turn into lakes.

All the way down the stairs, Sarah kept patting
Pat's arm and Pat kept moving away, keeping her
arm stiff.

"Watch out," she warned herself. "White kids
are all alike. Sarah's got something up her sleeve—
like the others."

Deborah stepped close, before she left the building. "If you feel bad," she said, "I could come back
from lunch early. We could talk."

"No," Pat snapped, and moved closer to Jo-Jo. Mrs. Klein, on the top of the landing, began to say something, looked at Pat, then stopped. She seemed to change her mind in mid-sentence. What came out was, "Come up with your friends after lunch. We'll be able to talk then."

Dumbly, Pat moved her head between a yes, a no, and a shrug.

Mrs. Klein walked to the lunch section of the indoor yard, greeted Lucy Mae, and repeated her invitation.

"She's nice," Lucy Mae said as Pat slid over to the center of the bench.

"I hate them all," Pat muttered.

Pat sat silently, gazing at her unopened lunch. Jo-Jo told Lucy Mae and the five other Negro children who shared their table what had happened in the classroom. "I didn't see who threw that spitball. It might have been Eric. When I find out, I'll fix him," Jo-Jo finished, brandishing his sandwich as if it were a weapon.

Then a general discussion began. Pat, sitting among classmates she could trust, who looked and talked like all her old friends, gradually thawed. The lump in her chest slowly dissolved.

Two boys were for ferreting out the enemy and "fixing his wagon." One boy joined the girls in insisting, "You can't fight them all."

Pat nodded. "That's right. My mother said that if we touch one of them, we'll have them all against us." She looked at Jo-Jo. "Did you see them this morning? It would have been a hundred against one."

She continued with a nervous giggle. "Imagine. They'd get us in a dark corner and . . . then they wouldn't be able to see us in the dark. They'd end up punching each other."

The tension at the table lifted for a moment.

Lucy Mae waited until the laughter stopped. In her quiet, serious voice, she asked, "What are we here for? To show who's stronger—whites or Negroes? Or to learn?"

"A lot I learned this morning," Pat and Jo-Jo said in chorus.

They stopped at the same time, then began again —together. Then Jo-Jo nodded to Pat. "You go ahead. You'll say it better, anyway," he said, and began to eat an apple.

Pat managed to bite into her sandwich. It became easier to swallow as she talked about the morning. "I was so busy trying to spot the kid who called us names that I missed everything Mrs. Klein said," Pat told them with a sigh. "And after I had studied my tables so good, too."

"Well, I was scared," Jo-Jo said, shoving wax

paper deep into his empty lunch bag. "Every second, I figured we would have to run for our lives."

"I'm asking my mother to take me out of here," a girl at the far end of the table cried. "I didn't want to come in the first place."

Pat made rabbit ears with her fingers and pulled the pretend rabbit under the table to hide. She had everyone smiling.

"Pat, this isn't funny," said Lucy Mae, slowly. "I like it when you make me laugh other times, but *this is not the time to joke!*"

Pat narrowed her eyes. She was a little angry. Usually she did as she chose. She met Lucy Mae's eyes. There was nothing in them but patience. Lucy Mae was not trying to take over or be boss. So, Pat decided to listen. She even smiled at Lucy Mae and Lucy Mae smiled back shyly.

Then Lucy Mae began to talk, and some of the students from other tables came over to listen.

"She's my friend," Pat told herself proudly.

Lucy Mae said seriously, "We can't run away. If *we* run, it will be bad for *all* Negroes, not just us."

"But what if we get chased?" Jo-Jo demanded. "Something tells me that Eric. . . ."

"We'll talk about Eric later," Lucy Mae broke in. "First we have to stay in school. And not to care what others say and do."

"And how are we going to do that?" a tall boy. asked. "Nobody in my class will even look me in the face."

There was more talk and some laughter. The teacher on duty came over and warned them to sit down and be quieter. Then he walked away. As the talk went on, no one questioned the wisdom of staying in the school.

The tall boy waved his hand. "Leave me out. I'm just minding my own business. You do what you want. I'm going out to play ball."

Pat didn't like that. It seemed an insult to Lucy Mae. "I want to listen to Lucy Mae's ideas," she said fiercely. Her enthusiasm affected the remaining children. "Lucy Mae knows about these things. Her father's a teacher."

That's when Lucy Mae began talking about the dramatic club and about the puppets. "My mother says if we join the club, we're sure to make friends. Two of the girls in Pat's class seem real friendly already."

Much as Pat hated to contradict Lucy Mae, she felt forced to. "Sarah? You think Sarah is really friendly? She may be only acting that way."

Lucy Mae shook her head. "Maybe. At least, Sarah and Deborah act friendly. If we go along with them, maybe we can make them *really* like us."

Jo-Jo threw his empty lunch bag into the garbage pail. "I think you're crazy. All white kids are like Eric. Say, want to see where he stuck me with his pencil?" He lifted his shirt sleeve and showed off a deep black mark. "The way he said he was sorry, I knew he done it on purpose."

"Did it," Lucy Mae corrected automatically, and Pat giggled.

The talk turned to the dramatic club again. Pat didn't see how a large membership would help the Negroes make friends. "If too many of us join, maybe all the whites will get out," she said, repeating talk she had heard at home.

Jo-Jo pushed his lip out to its furthest extent. "And what could I do in the club?"

"Thread needles," Pat said to Jo-Jo.

Lucy Mae answered. "What we do can be decided later. Now we have to find things that will make friends for us."

Pat said sadly, "My mother doesn't want me to join the club."

Lucy Mae and two other girls at their table wanted an explanation.

"Well, first my mother said that, with my father in the hospital, I ought to be ashamed of thinking about fun," Pat told them. "Next, that Sarah Mellon is a terror and she doesn't want me to hang around with terrors." Pat meant to be funny, and she succeeded. Even Lucy Mae laughed.

"How did your mother find out about Sarah?" Jo-Jo wanted to know.

"From your mother," Pat said. "She used to work for the Mellons."

Lucy Mae snapped her fingers. "I know why they say Sarah is a terror. Think of it, Pat. Didn't all the teachers in P.S. 27 say *you* were a terror? Why?"

"Cause I talked back to them and I always imitated them," Pat said without hesitation. Then she began to laugh. "Gosh. Maybe Sarah does the same thing. Maybe her mother won't want her to play with me because *I'm* a terror! And my mother doesn't want me to play with her because. . . ." and Pat giggled loudly.

Suddenly, she had to jump up. She had been still too long, frightened too long. She'd think of Negroes and Sarah and puppets some other time.

"Come on, Lucy Mae. Let's go, Jo-Jo. Race you to the street fence!" she sang out as she tossed her lunch bag right in the center of the trash basket.

chapter 9

By lunchtime Friday, Pat had run herself out. All she could think of was the puppet Sarah had helped her begin on Monday. Since Tuesday, the puppet had been on the back work table waiting for her.

"You run around the yard," Pat called to Jo-Jo. She reached for Lucy Mae's hand. "Want to come up to my room and work on our puppets?"

Lucy Mae smiled. "Mine will never be more than a roll of paper. But I'll come anyway."

Pat grinned. It was hard to imagine that a week ago, Lucy Mae had been a stranger.

The two girls went up the stairs and down the hall to Pat's room. Mrs. Klein had the door open.

She was sitting across the hall in another classroom, doing some work at a desk. She smiled when she saw them troop into the room and called out to them.

"Spread plenty of paper over the work table if you are going to make flour paste," she warned. She started to get out of her chair. "Do you want me in there?"

"We can manage," Pat said quickly. "We'll be careful. I'm good at cleaning up, my mother says."

She couldn't meet Mrs. Klein's eyes. The teacher seemed to be asking a question, a question about the other morning. But Pat wanted to forget what happened that morning and she certainly didn't want to talk about it.

Mrs. Klein went back to her work. She put Pat in charge until Sarah came. Pat wondered at this teacher who didn't seem worried about leaving children alone in the room. Mrs. Dillon would have been giving instructions and warnings every second.

While Lucy Mae tore newspaper into tiny strips, Pat found the string, cellophane tape, wire, and rolled-up papers from which the bodies and limbs of the puppets were to be made.

Her puppet was right where she had left it. A ball of paper was to be the head. The body was a folded and tied section of the *Times*. Long, dangling legs and arms hung through the folded loop of the body. Her fingers flew as she mixed the flour and water.

Deborah came running in as Pat began to wind the small wet strips of newspaper around the body.

"I went to call for Sarah. She lives on the fourth floor, I live on the sixth, but she wasn't ready. She's never ready—for important things," said Deborah when she caught her breath.

Pat barely looked up.

Just then, Phyllis, the brown-haired girl who, since the first day, had kept away from Pat, stuck her head in the door. "Where's Sarah? She wanted me to bring this wool." Out of her paper bag came a ball of shiny black wool.

Deborah gasped.

Pat looked up. "What's wrong?" she asked.

"Nothing," Deborah stammered, but her face called the word a lie.

Lucy Mae invited Phyllis to join them but the white girl snickered, "Me? I'm not—not a bus child!" She ran giggling down the hall.

Her visit left a dullness in the room. They all knew she had meant to insult them. Bus child. That was another way of saying Negro. Only the Negro children came to school on buses. The other children lived in the neighborhood and walked to school.

"We don't care," Deborah announced, "do we?"

Pat wanted to say, "Where do you get this *we* stuff?" but she fought the impulse. She gripped her puppet. "Don't you mind, Lucy Mae," she said. "You're better than she is."

"Sure thing!" Deborah affirmed passionately. "And better than that sneak, Sarah, too."

"Why do you talk that way about everybody? Sarah and Phyllis are your own kind!" Pat dropped her puppet on the table.

"They're *not* my kind," Deborah answered bitterly. "I moved in months ago. Nobody ever invites me to their houses. They all stick together. So, now I'm doing what my mother told me. I'm making *new* friends."

Lucy Mae stopped biting a hangnail. "But Sarah lives in your house, and she *seems* very friendly."

"Aw, Sarah. She's forever wanting to dress up. And she always wants to be the boss. She's your friend one day and not the next. When I moved in, she was really friendly. And now she won't even talk to me."

"Where is Sarah, anyway?" Pat asked. "I wish I lived near her. We'd have lots of fun."

"That's what you think," Deborah said mysteriously.

Pat shrugged and went on winding the strips of paper to make the body of her puppet. She already saw it painted a pale pink and white color, and she'd have the hair going in all directions, and a wide mouth with thin lips ready for talk or laughter. Maybe she'd call her puppet "Sar-occhio." Sarocchio could be a little girl without any real friends. She could go out into the world like Pinocchio and have adventures.

"Where *is* Sarah?" she asked again.

With her eyes saying more than her words, Deborah said, "Her mother was yelling at her when I went to her apartment. I heard her. She got paint all over the floor—*black paint.*"

Pat wondered why Deborah had made such a mystery of such an ordinary thing. Girls got paint on the floor and mothers scolded. So what?

Deborah looked toward the window. She had done little with her puppet since she came except turn it from side to side. "I'm going to make a fairy godmother puppet out of this," she said. "What's yours going to be?" she asked as Lucy Mae started to clear her table.

Lucy Mae laughed. "Bundle of old newspapers, I guess. My fingers just keep making messes."

Then Deborah said slowly, "I know what Sarah's puppet is going to be!"

"What?" asked Pat eagerly.

Deborah moved her shoulders from side to side. She wanted to be coaxed.

"Tell us," Lucy Mae said.

Pat didn't like the closed look on Deborah's face. "Let Sarah tell us when she comes," she said coldly.

Deborah sighed. She looked hurt. "You always act as if it's me who doesn't like you. I keep telling you, it's Sarah Mellon who doesn't."

"Prove it," Pat snapped. The puppet in her hand trembled. She thought, "I'm Negro, and some people may not like me for that, but I have friends. Nobody goes tattling about me." For the first time in her life, Pat was glad she wasn't white. Negro girls wouldn't tell tales about each other to white girls! She glared at Deborah.

Up went Deborah's chin. She squared her shoulders. "Ask Sarah what her puppet is going to be. I know. It's a black one. Black as coal. I told you Sarah makes fun of Negroes. Now you'll believe me."

Pat raised her hand. Phyllis and the jet-black wool—wool meant for a black doll's head. And black paint on the floor. Sarah *was* making a Negro puppet! Hadn't she put on black face to dance up the aisle during Brotherhood week. Deborah was telling the truth.

No sooner did Pat draw her hand back and admit Sarah's guilt than her thoughts went spinning in another direction. She stood, puppet in

hand, gnawing on her lip. Then it came to her—
a thought clear and bright.

Butterflies began fluttering under Pat's ribs. She
leaped up in the air, forgetting she was in a classroom, and cried, "Yipee!" She hugged her puppet,
threw her arms around Lucy Mae who stood wide-
eyed, and then hugged Deborah.

Deborah shook her head. "Crazy. The heat's gotten her."

Pat danced around the room hugging her puppet
and singing, "My buddy made a black puppet,
black puppet, black puppet. My buddy made a black
puppet just like *me*. I made a white puppet, white
puppet, white puppet. And I made a white puppet,
just like *she*."

Faces changed. Deborah turned from pale to red
to pale again. After a few awkward starts, she began
to laugh timidly. Lucy Mae joined her.

Lucy Mae said ruefully, "Going to a white school
has lots of surprises."

"Sure," said Pat in between giggles, "don't we
act different here, too? And other white girls surprise each other. Don't they, Debby?"

That was what she tried to explain to Carl that
night when she came down to help him sort the
old papers for the junk man. "You're wrong about
Sarah," she said. "She made a puppet like me, only

she made it beautiful. She brought it to school in the afternoon, though she was late. And it's the nicest puppet in the room. Debby thought she made it to make fun of me. But Carl, you ought to see it. I didn't know any white girl thought a Negro could look that nice!"

Carl shook his head and didn't say anything.

Later, when Mrs. Marley came home from the hospital, she heard about the day. But her main concern was with Pat's new-found friendship with Lucy Mae. "The Olivers are smart people. I'm glad that you and Lucy Mae are getting to be friends. But about that club. . . ."

"I know, I got to do my work in school. And home, too," said Pat. "But Ma, ask Papa. Ask him. Tell him how I don't answer back anymore." She grinned. "Tell him I'm too scared! But that I like my teacher."

"Write him a letter. You tell him. I'll do what he says." And those were the last words Mrs. Marley would say that night about the dramatic club application.

Pat finished her homework. She studied her five times table, and then wrote her letter. She had never before written a letter except in school. In school they began, "Dear Friend," or "Dear Mr. Marley." She tried Daddy. It was too babyish.

She decided to write just "Dear" and then tell him everything. *"I'm learning a lot,"* she wrote. *"White girls, some of them, are like Negro girls. But some are mean. I hate them. Lucy Mae says that I can help them like us. Can I join the club? The first meeting is the last Friday in September.*

And Sarah and me can maybe do a puppet show about a Negro girl and a white girl—only I'm sorry I made her ugly because she made me pretty. But Sarah's nice and she won't care. I like her and Mrs. Klein and Lucy Mae, and can I join the club for integration?"

She reread it. It was jumbled, but her father would understand. He always did.

chapter 10

The letter written, Pat sprinkled and rolled Carl's shirt into a moist ball. She wished her mother would get through bathing Ginny and sit down where they could talk. It was fine to want integration, but there were things about it that were scary.

One by one, the clothes for tomorrow were rolled and readied for ironing, and one by one, scary ideas came flying into Pat's mind.

Lucy Mae said that Sarah might be something like me, Pat mused. But was she? How would Sarah react when she found out that Pat's mother cleaned other people's houses? And Deborah? A white girl who told tales about another white girl! What would Deborah say about Pat when she found out?

"Ma, please can you come here a minute?" Pat begged.

"When the little ones are in bed," her mother answered, and Pat had to wait.

It took a long time. Willy wanted a song. Pat listened while she set up the ironing board. What song would her mother sing? If it was "Got The Whole World In His Hands," it meant that everything was fine. Mother was tired but feeling good. When she was low, she always sang "Jordan."

It was neither one, and Pat couldn't gauge her mother's mood. She locked the ironing board legs into place, keeping time with the singing.

How long had it been since her father's accident? Over a week! She had never spent a whole week without her father before. Right now, if her father were home, she would be telling him about the kids in class. She'd be able to tell him about Phyllis, the brown-haired girl in the back of the room. She'd be able to tell him how Eric bothered Jo-Jo. But she'd hold back about the spitball. Her father always got upset if someone hurt her.

Pat plugged in the iron and sighed. Nobody had a better father—or mother. When her mother came into the room, Pat said, "I'm glad you're my mother and not Mrs. Mellon."

While her mother put a chair near the ironing board so that she could sit as she worked, she asked Pat, "Why the sudden gladness?"

"Sarah's mother yelled like mad because of a little accident this noon," said Pat, embroidering on Deborah's story of the paint spilling.

"I'm not going to like working for a picky woman," Mrs. Marley said.

"Then don't go to work there," Pat cried, almost upsetting the ironing pile.

Her mother unfolded a shirt that Pat had washed and half-dried that afternoon. "Pat, you should be grown enough to understand that nobody has to be ashamed of honest work."

Pat looked uncomfortable. "I know, Ma. But it's hard to have my mother being like a slave for a girl in my class."

Mrs. Marley looked up sharply. "Where did you get this 'slave' business? And I thought you and this girl are friends." She stopped ironing and looked at Pat's stubborn face.

"Yes, but white girls are different. Most of my other friends have mothers who do the same work as you."

."How about Lucy Mae? Didn't you tell me a few days ago that you and Lucy Mae couldn't be friends —that she was too uppity for you? And now look

at you. Thick as thieves."

Her mother was right and Pat had no answer. But it didn't help any. It was all so mixed up.

On line the next morning, Sarah was full of an argument with her mother about the puppet. "She wants me to quit playing with dolls. She says I'm too big."

Jo-Jo leaned across the line. "So, how come she signed your club application?"

Sarah twirled her hair. "It helps in junior high. It goes on your service record. My brother Arnie had been stage manager for Mrs. Klein since fourth grade. My mother had better sign my application or I'll run away and *never* come back." The words all came out in a rush.

The dramatic club, Pat learned from Sarah, was for the whole school. Anyone from fourth grade up could join. Meetings were once a week after school from three until five o'clock.

"The best thing is the P.T.A. meetings," Sarah whispered, going up the stairs. "Every month at P.T.A. meetings, we get to take care of the children. We have shows for them—wow!"

"My mother hasn't signed my slip yet," was all Pat could say.

Right after lunch, Sarah ran through the indoor yard to the lunch tables. "Coming, Pat? I got to get my hands on a big glob of paste. I'm going to make a ball as big as my fist and then I'm going to throw it at the wall or jump on it."

"What's bothering you?" Pat asked as she tossed her lunch bag away. She was getting used to Sarah's ways of getting rid of her frequent spells of anger.

"My brother Arnie and my mother!" said Sarah.

"So? What's new about that?"

Jo-Jo snapped his fingers. "If I had a sister like you, I'd tear my hair. I don't blame them, whatever happened."

"What did I do?" Sarah practically screamed. "Is it my fault I tripped over his old football? No! But I'm the one she blames."

Pat ran ahead. Over her shoulder, she said, "I'm glad my mother doesn't nag me. And my brother Carl—say, if I wanted him to do anything for me. . . ." she hugged herself. "I love all my brothers."

Sarah was right behind her on the steps. They ran into the classroom, and Sarah made a dash for the flour. "And all I hear all day and night is 'Watch out! Watch out!'" Sarah imitated her mother's voice and made a face. "Let me make a ball and squash it before I bu-u-ust!"

Two seconds later, Sarah and Pat were talking calmly about their puppets. Deborah hadn't come back early, so the two girls worked alone. Lucy Mae was trying to find a fairy tale book in the library to check the spelling of Pinocchio's name. Sarah and Pat were planning some adventures similar to Pinocchio's for their puppet play.

"Gosh, it's fun working with you," Sarah sighed, as the bell rang.

"Best fun I've ever had in school," Pat said, as she cleaned up. She kept Sarah from helping. "You always spill the water. Let me do it. I'm faster!"

To Sarah's question of why she was good at cleaning up, Pat answered, "Because I do it so often." She hoped Sarah would question her some more. Then, maybe, she could sneak in the information that her mother would be working for Sarah's mother. She was embarrassed about it, but she knew she had to tell Sarah just in case someone else—like Phyllis, maybe—tried to tell her first. And Phyllis would be sure to tell it so it would sound awful. If Pat told Sarah herself, she'd first talk about "the dignity of all honest work," the way her mother had.

The right moment finally came to tell Sarah, but Sarah wouldn't stop talking. As each child came into class, Sarah called out, "Hey, that Pat is a whiz! You ought to see the way she cleans up!"

Phyllis walked in with some friends. In a nasty voice that carried, although she whispered it to her companions, she said, "What's surprising? My mother says all of *them* are good at that!"

Pat felt her cheeks grow hot. She squeezed the sponge in her hand extra hard to keep her hands from hitting out at Phyllis' smiling face. All thought of telling Sarah was gone. Maybe cleaning house *was* honest work but, somehow, she felt that telling Sarah now would only serve to prove Phyllis' point.

chapter 11

On Friday, the day of the first meeting of the dramatic club, Pat was miserable. She had grown more and more uneasy as the arrangements were made.

Her father had given his reluctant consent. Mrs. Meadows, who worked the late shift in the store on Fridays, was taking care of Ginny. The twins were going to help Carl and Junior collect and tie the old newspapers for the ragman. Mrs. Marley was going to work for the Mellons and at five—when the meeting was over—would meet Pat, Lucy Mae, and Jo-Jo at the main entrance to the school.

"Rush hour is no time for children to be traveling alone," the grownups had said. And no one had been the least inclined to argue.

"Huh!" Jo-Jo said as he balanced his books on his head. "I could be playing ball with the boys instead. How did I get roped into this thing anyway?"

"Sarah will be there, and you can count on her not to make it a strictly girl-type thing," Lucy Mae said sternly. "You think she's fun, don't you?"

Jo-Jo let both hands go and held the pose, while the bus joggled the books on his head. "Because she's not always talking about *things*!" Jo-Jo made no pretense of liking all the talk about integration. He only came up to the classrooms during lunch recess when Sarah was around because, with Sarah there, there was always lots of laughter.

"Pat acts like she used to in P.S. 27 when Sarah is around," he declared, and both Pat and Lucy Mae knew this was true.

Pat changed the subject to something that was worrying her. "Are you sure this club is a good idea?" Pat asked Lucy Mae as she edged her way around towards a pole.

"Well. . . ." Pat saw the raw skin around Lucy Mae's thumbnail where she had chewed on it. She knew Lucy Mae was as worried as she.

"Well," Lucy Mae repeated, "Barbara is coming, and that makes four of *us*. It can't be any worse than the first day of school when we didn't know a soul. And we lived through that!"

Four Negroes and forty-two white children. Pat shook her head. She didn't like the odds. And, too, among the forty-two were several from her class that she knew would be unfriendly. With Phyllis around, no meeting could possibly be fun.

"And Sarah is going to be there," Lucy Mae said to Pat, just as she had to Jo-Jo.

"What makes you think Sarah is going to talk to me after today?" Pat asked.

"Didn't you tell her yet?" Lucy Mae asked. "You promised to tell about your mother, yesterday. So she would know ahead of time. What are you afraid of?"

What *was* she afraid of? Pat shook her head. Her misery grew. She reviewed her relationship with the white girl. Since the day that Sarah had brought in her black puppet, she had grown to like Sarah more and more. She remembered Jo-Jo asking, over Lucy Mae's protests, "Sarah, what was your Mother yelling at you about? Doesn't she want you sitting next to one of us?"

Sarah had looked puzzled. "How would she know?" Sarah had answered. "I never told her about it. Besides, she just doesn't like black paint on the floor. And she's afraid that if I make a black puppet some . . ." Sarah wrinkled her nose, "some Negro in school might see it and get mad and maybe get a gang after me. Isn't that funny? You wouldn't do that, would you?"

Pat had told her mother all about that scene. "Sarah meant the puppet to be beautiful," she had explained. "She likes me, I'm sure. But, even though she likes us, she really thinks, like her mother, that maybe we *will* gang up on her. Isn't that queer?"

"What are you afraid of?" Lucy Mae asked again, bringing Pat back to the present problem of telling Sarah about her mother.

Jo-Jo stuck his head between the two girls, "Sarah sure isn't scared of you. She babbles about her family like a fountain."

"This morning I'll tell her," Pat promised.

Talking to Lucy Mae and Jo-Jo made her fears seem empty. Then she thought, *how would I feel if she told me her mother was going to work for my mother?* The answer was obvious. It wouldn't matter in the least.

"I'll tell her as soon at I see her."

She didn't!

Jo-Jo saw Sarah coming with Deborah. He called across the indoor yard, "Hey, Sarah, Pat wants to tell you a secret!"

Pat's eyes lashed him, but he hooted, and ran for cover in the boys' line. With Deborah standing there, Pat was not going to say any more than "Hi."

In the general whispering, while sweaters were being put in the closet and books were put away, Pat tried to tell Sarah. Unsuccessfully. Sarah was full of complaints about Deborah, who had called for her and somehow informed Mrs. Mellon that Sarah had done a division example on the board—all wrong.

"I *told* my mother that I get mixed up when I go to the board. But does that make any difference? No! All she talks about is putting me in a school where there is less play and more work. Can you beat that?" Sarah asked.

Pat met Jo-Jo's questioning eyes and shook her head. *This* was no time for confessions.

During arithmetic, she and Sarah were separated. Pat and Jo-Jo were in the remedial arithmetic group, getting drilled in number combinations. Ten minutes every morning the remedial group worked while the rest of the class had a library period. Mrs. Klein called the numbers "sight numbers" and Pat discovered that eight and seven together soon became a sight number for her. One look, and she wrote fifteen. The ten minutes usually flew too fast, but today they were endless.

Back in her seat correcting homework, Pat found a note from Sarah. It read *"Maybe today I can come back to school by twelve fifteen. Try to eat fast. We'll try out our play."*

Pat sneaked a glance at the back counter where several puppets were laid out. Her poodle-haired one needed a touch of paint for the lips and ribbons for the dress. The hollow head had been tested. Her hand fitted comfortably inside and the dress sleeves were the right length for her fingers.

The black-faced puppet was ready, too. Sarah wanted to make braids instead of smooth waves. "I think your braids look as nice as Lucy Mae's pony tail," she had said. But Pat dissuaded her. Sarah couldn't promise that black wool braids wouldn't make the class laugh, and it had been agreed that only the poodle-haired doll was to be the laugh-getter.

"Well?" Sarah whispered.

Pat nodded. The black puppet sitting against the wall made her feel guilty. Sarah had proved her friendship, but was Pat going to prove hers? She was about to tell Sarah her secret at that moment, but Mrs. Klein began teaching how to add fractions and Pat didn't dare look away from the board.

"Sarah," Mrs. Klein's voice cracked sharply, "How many eighths in one-fourth of this apple?"

Jo-Jo was social studies book monitor and, as he passed her desk at quarter of eleven, he asked, under his breath, "Did you?" When she shook her head, he leaned over and whispered, "If she gets mad at Lucy Mae and me, I'll flatten your ears!"

"What's up?" Deborah asked. Sarah had dropped her loose-leaf notebook and was under the desk picking up the papers. Pat slumped down in her seat. Jo-Jo had every right to be angry. Sarah might take it out on Jo-Jo and Lucy Mae. Wouldn't she, Pat Marley, react that way? *If only,* Pat prayed to herself, *there was no club meeting today for some reason. Any reason.* Or maybe she could get sick and Jo-Jo and Lucy Mae would have to take her home early. Then Sarah wouldn't see her mother at school and find out who the new cleaning lady was.

Wishing helped her keep her book steady. She was on a committee with Sarah, Deborah, and two boys. For homework, they had to ask their parents and grandparents why they had immigrated to the United States. Pat knew her answers without asking. Her father had come to New York from North Carolina when he was eighteen. Her mother's people had come North when she was eight. Where they had come from before they had lived in North Carolina, Pat had heard about too often to forget. It was part of her skin, part of her heartbeats. Nobody talked about it—but everybody knew.

She listened to the other children making plans.

"I'm going to make a diorama to show my grand-mother's village in Poland," the freckle-faced boy said. "Could you help me with the doll's faces?" he asked Pat.

Pat was about to answer when Sarah interrupted. "Maybe me and Pat can make a slave ship. My puppet will be the slave girl."

Pat whispered viciously, "Just because your puppet's black doesn't mean she's a slave."

The criticism was unfair and Pat knew it. The committee was interested in showing the rest of the class how Americans had first come to the country. And some—mostly Negroes—had come in slave ships. But thinking about her heritage in that light made it impossible to tell Sarah about her mother.

A dozen times during the committee meeting she saw Jo-Jo motion, and she had to shake her head. *Maybe after lunch,* she said to herself, and tried to concentrate on the plans with the others.

During social studies project time lots of movement and giggling was to be expected. Pat's group whispered and worked on their "immigration" ideas. Pat helped the freckle-faced boy with his figures for the diorama.

Mrs. Klein was working with the "explorer" committee, two seats away. These were the boys and girls who would be reporting about the first men who traveled the wilderness of America.

Pat was working so hard on the heads of the Polish figures, she barely heard the giggling increase. Sarah was sitting next to her, engrossed in a picture from an old magazine showing a slave ship and its passengers.

Mrs. Klein looked up. "What's going on back there?" she asked when the giggling from the back of the room persisted.

Pat glanced back and saw nothing unusual. Phyllis and Eric and others were together near the sink. Probably just getting in line to wash up. But there was something about the giggling that made Pat squirm up against the back of her seat.

Again the noise broke out, but Mrs. Klein's sharp command to sit down and get to work had its effect.

Sarah looked up from the picture and called out, "May I get my puppet, Mrs. Klein? I need to make a different dress for it for my project."

Before Mrs. Klein could nod, Pat heard suppressed gasps and heads turned her way briefly. No one met her eyes. The noise increased.

Sarah was halfway to the counter. Phyllis' and Eric's eyes were on Sarah's back—or something right beyond it. Pat's skin suddenly felt as if it had turned to sandpaper.

Sarah let loose a howl and Pat held her breath.

She knew, somehow, that howl had something to do with her. Something awful was happening. Pat stood up.

"Look!" Sarah screamed, and held up her puppet. But it wasn't her puppet any more. The dress had been torn off, and a brown body replaced it. A monkey's body made out of a paper bag. All the

black wool had been taken from the head, leaving the skull bare except for two monkey ears which had been pinned on. The beautiful black girl was gone. An impish paper-bag monkey had taken its place.

"Look!" screamed Sarah again. "Phyllis did that!"

"So what? It's only a puppet," Phyllis answered.

Pat stood frozen. Her body had become heavy. Why did Phyllis hate her so? What had she done to anyone in this room that they should want to hurt her? Perspiration formed on her face, her back, her legs.

"*Only* a puppet?" Sarah said. "But it's mine— and you spoiled it. You. . . ." Sarah's hands jerked up into the air. She was close to Phyllis and her blows landed on the seated girl's head and shoulders.

"Sarah!"

Mrs. Klein's voice unleashed Pat's legs. With a smothered cry, she ran to Sarah. Whether to help her or to stop her wasn't clear.

"Patricia!"

"Get her, Pat!" She thought it was Jo-Jo calling, and she gritted her teeth. *Let Lucy Mae worry about integration. Pat Marley was through being made fun of.*

She reached beyond Sarah's shoulder. Her weight was behind her arm. She landed a blow on Phyllis' back just as her hand was gripped from behind.

"I don't blame you for being angry," Mrs. Klein said. "We're all angry. Phyllis ought to be ashamed of herself." Mrs. Klein held tightly to Pat's arm. "Let's sit down and talk about this. This is serious."

Pat thought she heard people running. But it was only her heartbeats. Then she was in her seat, Sarah's hand, damp and hot, was inside her own. Her other hand seemed on fire. She looked at it. It ached from being clenched too long. Slowly, she loosened her fist.

Mrs. Klein's voice was uneven. "Phyllis, you must talk first. What did Patricia and Sarah do to you to make *you* do such a senseless, cruel thing?"

Words came pouring out of Phyllis. She hadn't done it alone. It had been a joke. Didn't she have the right to make a joke?

"Have you the right to touch another person's work?"

"No."

"Have you the right to make fun of anyone?"

"No—but Sarah and Pat aren't holy."

"Will someone comment on what Phyllis said?"

From under her lashes, Pat saw hands go slowly up in the air. Were they going to help her? Mrs. Klein had helped. Pat heard the change in the breathing behind her. There was no laughter now. Mrs. Klein was obviously on her side. Would the class be?

A blond girl in the center aisle was the first to talk. "We're all to blame. I'm ashamed. Pat's all right. She doesn't hurt us any. And Sarah and

Deborah keep telling us that if we give Pat a chance, she's loads of fun. I'm sorry, Pat." The girl sat down.

Mrs. Klein obviously agreed with the girl. Pat knew that others would talk up now. They did.

Others took the blame. And Pat knew that many who didn't talk up were sorry. She heard paper being torn and felt a bit of tissue pressed into her hand.

"Thanks," she whispered, holding tight to Sarah's hand. Sarah had torn the tissue awkwardly with her free hand and had passed it to Pat. They were both sniffling.

"Siamese twins," Sarah whispered.

Pat heard more talk going on about her, and she sniffed her tears to a stop. Some word had to be said. Pat took a deep breath. After all, some of it was her fault, too. In some way, it was her fault. Here Sarah was the best friend she had ever had, but did Pat trust her? Deborah, too. And lots of the others were her friends. She had to say something.

Up went Pat's free hand. "I'm sorry I hit Phyllis," she said. "And I'm not angry about the giggling. Me and Sarah like people to laugh, I guess." She ended haltingly.

Mrs. Klein gave the class a minute to recover before she began to talk. "I'll expect some fine performances from this class, and especially from this great little team," she said, nodding at Pat and Sarah. "I hope they'll both be able to stay for our first club meeting this afternoon. After the sample of sportsmanship we just saw, I hope more of you will bring in signed applications after lunch."

Pat held her breath. She didn't know whether to laugh or cry. She was happy to have found out she had friends. But here it was almost lunch and she still hadn't told Sarah about her mother! Sarah would go home for her meal and find Pat's mother cleaning up. And—why couldn't her tongue say the necessary words? Apologizing to Phyllis had been possible—and she hated Phyllis. Why couldn't she tell Sarah?

Pat buried her head in a book and pushed her thoughts aside. There was still a little time.

chapter 12

For awhile, it looked as if Pat might not get to tell
Sarah at all that day. No sooner did the lunch bell
ring than a dozen or more girls suddenly seemed
to have errands on Pat's side of the room.

Pat realized almost instantly that the errands were
faked. They were all excuses to come to Pat and
Sarah and whisper. The words hardly mattered.
They all said almost the same thing.

"That Phyllis is a pill. Never mind what she
says!"

Pat listened and her eyes shone. Her smile grew
wider and wider.

Deborah looked at her with admiration. "I'd

never have been able to act as brave as you," she said.

It was a miracle that, with all the movement and the whispering, and Sarah sliding in and out of her chair because she was so nervous, Mrs. Klein didn't say anything. She just waited until the noise died down and the children were all seated. Then she gave the order to line up for lunch dismissal.

Pat was exhausted by the time she got on line behind Deborah and ahead of Sarah. Jo-Jo was right next to her.

"What did they all want?" Jo-Jo nudged and asked, without making a sound. His eyes formed the question.

It was impossible for Pat to answer. The day had suddenly exploded. A beautiful, good explosion with gorgeous colors and lots of music. The sound of feet on the stairs was a symphony such as she'd heard last year in a special music assembly. The shadows on the steps disappeared as soon as she rounded each corner. She forgot the horror of Phyllis' prank, remembering only the support of the class.

Why had she imagined that white faces looked alike? Why had Junior told her all white kids had to be watched? Why had her father worried about them being nasty to her?

"Let's eat and get outside," Pat called happily

as she ran to her table. She couldn't eat fast enough. Lucy Mae and Barbara wanted to hear over and over again what Phyllis had done and said. They wanted her to repeat what the other children had said and what Mrs. Klein had said. Out of doors, Lucy Mae, Jo-Jo, and Pat joined hands. They spun around and around as fast as their feet would go. Barbara and the other lunch children watched them and laughed.

"We're filled with laughing gas!" Pat shouted. "Come and join us. Wheee—we're on our way to the moon."

In class, notes came rushing in. Temma wanted to know if Sarah's mother minded other children coming over. She wanted to help make the puppet beautiful again. Sarah pursed her lips after reading that one. She couldn't contain herself long enough to write an answer. She turned around in her seat and whispered loudly, "Temma! Temma, thanks. But my mother doesn't even let me bring a drop of paste in the house anymore."

"Then come to my house," Pat interrupted.

Sarah looked surprised. Pat looked back, equally surprised. She hadn't known she was going to say that! It was an unspoken understanding that the neighborhood children didn't go across town to the homes of the bus children. No one said so—it was simply understood.

Once said, the idea appealed to Pat. But Mrs. Klein was tapping her desk with a ruler and looking hard at Pat. Pat looked back. Mrs. Klein didn't look really angry.

"Mrs. Klein, I just want to invite Sarah to my house to fix her puppet. My mother won't care if we make a mess. I can do the cleaning up."

"That's a nice thought, Patricia. We'll talk about it after school," Mrs. Klein answered.

"But there's club meeting after school," Sarah interrupted. "Mrs. Klein, do you think I can go?" Sarah's eyes were double their size and neither her hands nor her feet seemed able to stay put. "Can *you* make my mother let me go?"

Mrs. Klein refused to discuss the invitation; it was time for the class to begin work.

After school, at the first club meeting, there was a lot of talk about the P.T.A. and the club's job of baby sitting for the younger children. Then, plans were made for the shows that were to be given.

At the end of the meeting, Jo-Jo helped to put the chairs back in the rooms they had come from. Pat helped Sarah get things together for some of the new members who wanted to make puppets at home over the weekend. Debby and Lucy Mae washed the blackboards.

Mrs. Klein stopped for an instant near Sarah and Pat. "Sarah, why don't you ask your mother if she will allow you to eat lunch in school next week. Then you and Patricia can eat here and work on your puppets."

"Oh, yes—do," said Pat enthusiastically. "But— I still want you to come to my house. My mother has a sewing machine and we can make the new dress for the puppet on it. It would be super!"

Sarah threw her arms around Pat first, and then Mrs. Klein. "The lunch part's okay," she said. "I know that without asking. But will you write my mother about going to Pat's house?" she begged Mrs. Klein.

Pat understood the agony in Sarah's voice. Without being told, she knew that Mrs. Mellon would object to having her daughter ride into the Negro part of the school district. Unless, perhaps, Mrs. Klein said it was all right.

"Please help Sarah visit me," Pat added her plea to Sarah's, but in a much lower voice.

Jo-Jo, carrying a chair over his head, added helpfully, "Sarah's mother ought to trust Pat's mother. She trusts her to. . . ."

"*Jo-Jo*" screamed Pat, shaking with anger. "Bigmouth. When'll you ever learn?"

Mrs. Klein's arm rose softly, quickly, drew Pat over, and quieted her. "Finish getting the chairs where they belong, Johnny," she said gently. "Sometimes girls need to be alone."

She shooed Sarah and Pat behind the puppet stage and asked them to wait for her. In less than three minutes, Mrs. Klein had the room in order, the club members on line and ready to leave. "Deborah and Lucy Mae, will you lead the line down? I'll meet you at the door in a moment."

Jo-Jo was with them, and she smiled broadly at him. "Patricia will be down in a minute."

The other children filed out of the room, and Mrs. Klein turned to Pat "Is there something we ought to know, Patricia? Johnny seemed to want to help."

Pat sniffled. Mrs. Klein's eyes were questioning gently. By some miracle, Sarah was sitting still and silent. Suddenly it didn't seem terribly hard to say, "My mother is cleaning for Sarah's mother today."

Sarah looked startled. "What did you say?"

Pat sniffed, looked up at Mrs. Klein who nodded, and repeated to Sarah, "My mother is working for your mother today. In your house. And she's downstairs now waiting for me."

"But your mother is *not* at my house," Sarah said in confusion. "Only a new girl is there, a nice one named Eulalie. It's a funny name, isn't it? But she's a nice girl."

"She's not a girl. She's my mother and her name is Mrs. Marley," Pat retorted.

Mrs. Klein's arm was steady around Pat's shoulder. "Sarah didn't mean to be rude, Pat. It's what some people call their cleaning ladies."

"But why is your mother cleaning my house." Sarah asked uncomprehendingly. "Is it for the P.T.A. or something?"

Pat couldn't understand Sarah's confusion. She said very distinctly and slowly, "That's my mother's work. She cleans people's houses for money." She said it clearly as though she were speaking to someone hard of hearing. She watched Sarah carefully, but could make nothing of what Sarah's face was showing. Surprise. Shock. Disbelief.

"Really? Is that her work?" She looked at Pat. "Are you poor?"

Pat shrugged. "Maybe—I don't know." She turned to Mrs. Klein again. "Am I?" She didn't actually know what being "poor" was. The Marleys had little money, but were they *poor*?

"I guess not, Pat," Mrs. Klein said. "Have you a father? Brothers? A sister? A mother who cares enough for you to stand outside the school waiting to take you home?"

Pat nodded at each question.

"Then you're not poor!" Mrs. Klein answered promptly.

"More than mine would do," Sarah mumbled enviously.

"My father's not around now," Pat added. "He's in the hospital getting his broken hip fixed."

She felt Sarah's hand creep into hers and Mrs. Klein's arm leave her shoulder at the same time. "That's why my mother's got to work every day— there's doctor's bills and hospital bills and things."

"I'm sorry I didn't clean my room better," Sarah said. "Gee, your poor mother must be tired after cleaning up my mess. My mother always complains after *she* does the job."

Hand in hand, Pat and Sarah started out of the room. Mrs. Klein turned out the light and followed them down the stairs where the rest of the club members were waiting for them.

Once outside, they saw Mrs. Marley. Pat ran to her mother.

"Next week you needn't come all the way here to meet the children," Mrs. Klein said to Mrs. Marley. "Pat told me you were working in the Mellon house, and that's right on our way to the bus. I can bring the children to you while you sit in the lobby of the building."

Mrs. Marley didn't answer, but she smiled and nodded.

Sarah came up to Mrs. Marley and called her by name. "Mrs. Marley, I'll try not to leave my room so messy. And please, can I come and visit Pat some day soon?"

Again Mrs. Marley nodded. "Don't worry your little head none about the mess. I've seen worse. Anyway, cleaning is my job."

"But can she come?" Pat begged.

Mrs. Marley looked sideways at Mrs. Klein. Then she answered quietly, "If Sarah's mother *says* she can come."

Pat and Sarah dropped back into the group, but not so far as to miss a word of what Mrs. Klein was saying. She was telling Mrs. Marley about Pat's talent as an actress. Pat couldn't hear enough of that. She pinched herself to keep from leaping into the air. But then came topics not so flattering— arithmetic, mainly.

"Patricia should spend more time studying her multiplication tables," Mrs. Klein said. "Does she have a good place to study?"

That made Mrs. Marley tell her about Mr. Marley's accident. "Patricia is working like a grownup—cleaning up, and taking care of her brothers and sisters. Even cooking. It's a wonder she finds any time at all to study."

Pat wanted to hug her mother. She sounded so proud.

"And, up to now," continued Mrs. Marley, "Patricia didn't need any special place to study. She hated anything that had to do with school." Mrs. Marley ended with a chuckle. "When her Pa gets home, I guess he'll fix her a desk—now that she needs one."

They left Mrs. Klein at the corner. She took a bus going in the opposite direction. All the children who had walked with them had already been deposited at their various doorsteps.

Pat couldn't stop talking about her day. When was her father going to build a desk? When was he coming home?

"Maybe up until now you didn't miss him," Mrs. Marley teased. "Now, cause you want a desk, you're itching to see him!" But she said that he would be home in eight or ten days. "He won't be able to walk," Mrs. Marley warned. "Not even on crutches. He'll have to have one of those chairs you stand up in."

Pat hugged her mother. She was so pleased a date

had been set for her father's home-coming. That good news, on top of all the things that had happened that day, made her want to dance all the way home.

chapter 13

For the next week, Pat went about in a whirl of rainbows. It didn't bother her when Junior, at the dinner table one night, spoofed her intention of having Sarah visit.

"Sarah has already told her mother about me!" Pat stated emphatically. "I just know she has. After all, I've told you all about her."

"Wanna bet?" asked Junior, and Carl took his side.

No matter how many times Mrs. Marley said, "Children, eat and be quiet" Pat couldn't keep from springing up and shouting, "I know Sarah better'n you. She can't keep her mouth shut for a minute. She's as bad as Jo-Jo. So there!"

But she didn't win the argument. Mrs. Marley took the older boys' side. "Sometimes, Pat, a girl who talks a lot knows when to keep her mouth shut. I've known lots of big talkers who know when not to talk!"

"But I've *got* to have Sarah here. I want her to see the twins and Pa. I want to have everybody meet her." Pat's voice developed a whine.

No one said anything after that. They just looked down into their dinner plates and ate in silence.

After dinner, when Pat rose to help her mother do the dishes, Mrs. Marley pushed Pat towards the other room. "Tonight, honey, you go do home-work. In a few more days, Papa will be home. You and Papa together, maybe you can think of some way to get Sarah here. You two have the brains of the family. Now you got more than a desk you want your pa for, huh, Pat?"

Then, soapy hands and all, she pulled Pat into her arms and held her fast. "You'll find a way, honey. I'm sure of it."

Mrs. Marley's confidence wasn't misplaced. The closer her father's home-coming got, the harder Pat worked at home and at school—and the more she wracked her brain for ways to prove to Mrs. Mel-lon that Sarah was safe in a Negro child's home.

She thought of having Lucy Mae's father, who was a teacher, pick Sarah up. But before she even asked, she dismissed the idea as impractical and, somehow, dishonest. She wanted her house and her family liked for what *they* were, not what Lucy Mae's father was.

"Ask your mother," she begged Sarah again on the Thursday before her father was due home. The girls were putting the finishing touches on Sarah's rebuilt puppet; they had been working on the puppet every lunch hour for over a week.

"You crazy?" Sarah jumped up and the bottle of black paint overturned. "Oh—just like at home," she said and kept hopping about.

Pat had paper towels around the mess almost instantly, and she motioned for Sarah to get more. Sarah went over to the cabinet. She didn't stop talking the whole time. "You know my mother won't let me cross town. She's even afraid to let me go on the avenue alone."

"Why the avenue?" Pat had all the paint blotted up. Carefully, she brought the wastebasket to the table and tucked the dirty towels in clean towels before putting them inside.

"You know why," Sarah said, with a meaningful toss of her head.

Puzzled, Pat asked. "Why?"

"Because there are Negro people on the other side

of the avenue and my mother says it's dangerous to go walking alone."

"But I don't live across the avenue. I live across town," Pat explained. "And you only have to walk to your corner and then take the bus. Fifteen cents carfare and then you are at my house."

Pat started to put away the supplies. "I've got an idea," she said casually, though she had been planning to say it all day. "Why don't you come on Saturday. We're having a party for my father—a home-coming party. Everyone in the building is coming to see my father. We want to show him how glad we are he's home."

Sarah ignored the invitation. "Why doesn't your mother save the money for the party and buy you a new coat instead. You need it," she said as she put the box of pins in the sewing basket with a flourish.

Pat was used to Sarah's frankness. She answered honestly. "The best present is having my father home. Who cares about an old coat. I'll make believe my last year's is supposed to be a long jacket."

"You'd better get a coat this year," said Sarah, doggedly sticking to the subject. "You're still wearing a sweater. If it was me, I'd be frozen so stiff I couldn't walk!"

Pat shrugged. It was a subject *she'd* rather not

talk about. She had to get Sarah back on the subject of the party. "You could come," she said. "You
could slip out of the house and pretend you're going to Debby's or somewhere and you could be
across town in half an hour. We could do our puppet show. My father would love it. And, after you
were there, your mother couldn't *really* be mad. I
mean, after all, my mother works for your mother.
It isn't as if she doesn't know us."

Sarah turned a funny color. "I—I didn't tell my
mother."

"You didn't tell her about my mother being your
cleaning lady?" Pat whispered hoarsely.

Sarah shook her head.

"Why not?" Pat demanded.

"If she finds out about you, she'll—she'll make
me stop being your friend. A colored boy once took
my brother's pen. Since then, my mother thinks
every colored kid is going to steal my things, or
beat me up or something."

Pat wet her lips so they wouldn't stiffen and refuse to talk. Not that there was anything to say.

"Honest, Pat, I don't feel that way. Only, my
mother does. I mean, what can I do?"

Pat wanted to lash out against Sarah's mother.
But Sarah was her friend. Friends didn't say things
against one another's mothers. She could only brag

about her relatives to point out the differences between the families.

"You can come to my house. You'll see how nice my brothers are. Even the twins. They helped me me wash every window in the apartment the other day. Frankie held my feet so I wouldn't feel wobbly and Willy, he cleaned the insides while I cleaned the outsides." Pat kept talking, hoping, somehow, to convince Sarah.

"I'd like to come to your house, honest," said Sarah with a sigh. "But I couldn't get the thirty cents to get there and back. I'd have to walk."

"Funny, isn't it," Pat said slowly. "Lucy Mae's mother keeps talking about integration. She keeps telling Lucy Mae that all we have to do is to let the white children get to know us. Yet, you know me and we want to visit each other's houses, but your mother won't let you. Seems like what we *really* ought to do is let the grownups get to know each other."

But there was no time to figure out the carfare. It was almost time for class to begin, and Pat had to get ready for the spelling test. To Pat, the test was extra important. She wanted her father to see a passing mark. On last week's test, she had gotten four wrong—not quite passing. This week, she had had Lucy Mae quiz her all the way to school each morning. The test, right now, was even more important than the party. That, at least, could wait.

On the way home, she told Lucy Mae and Jo-Jo that she had asked Sarah to come to the party *without* permission. And that Sarah hadn't told her mother—at least not just yet—about Mrs. Marley.

"But why should you teach Sarah to lie to her mother?" Lucy Mae asked, when she heard Pat's plan. "And where will you get the bus fare?"

"That's not really lying," Jo-Jo said staunchly. "It's just not saying." *He* knew the money was the least of the problem.

"That's the same thing," Lucy Mae insisted.

But Pat and Jo-Jo talked very loudly and soon Lucy Mae kept quiet.

"Only, don't say anything to your folks," Pat cautioned. "Not that they ought to mind. They're the ones who keep on saying that we'll be friends with the white kids soon. Well, I'm making sure that what they say comes true. Sarah will come over. She'll like us and then go home and tell her mother there's no cause to be scared of Negroes. Isn't that right?"

Lucy Mae was finally convinced, or at least she didn't say anything more against the idea. To Pat, it was the same thing. But the carfare money still remained a problem.

"I could ask my mother for a dollar," said Lucy Mae. "It's really my own money. I've been saving for an autograph book."

Both Jo-Jo and Pat agreed that it was better to find the fare elsewhere. Asking Mrs. Oliver would be dangerous.

"I'd give it to you if I had it," Jo-Jo said, but of course, he didn't have it.

And Pat didn't either.

That night, Pat thought of asking her mother for it. But she took one look at her mother's drawn face and decided not to. Seeing how tired her mother looked, Pat said nothing. Instead, she rapidly unpacked all the groceries and put them away.

By the time homework was done and the last dish was washed and returned to its place on the shelf, Pat had almost given up on the carfare problem. Junior and Carl came in late, and Pat was almost asleep when Carl dropped into his bed.

"I made an extra dollar and fifteen cents," he whispered. "I want to get Papa a special present. Got any ideas, Pat?"

Pat was wide awake instantly. She leaned way over the side of the bed and brought her head as close to his as possible. Her heart was beating double time. "Carl, Carl, I got a special present to give Papa."

"What?" Carl sat up in bed.

"Sarah! Give Sarah thirty cents and she'll come to the party. Papa will be surprised!"

"I bet," said Carl under his breath, but didn't say anything more.

When Carl didn't continue, Pat began to talk faster. "And then, Sarah and me, we'll bring out our puppets and Papa will see a real puppet show. How about that? Won't that be a surprise and a present?"

Carl asked her with intensity, "Did you get Mrs. Mellon to say yes? Did you?"

Pat brushed his arms aside. "No," she whispered, careful to avoid Junior's entrance into the discussion. Then, with infinite gentleness, she stroked her brother's hand. "Carl, listen to me," she begged. "How is Mrs. Mellon ever going to find out we're nice if she never lets Sarah come here?"

At last, almost as if he simply wanted to get to sleep, he sighed. "It's you I'm giving the present to—because you worked harder than all the rest of us—what with going to school with white kids and getting good marks and cooking and cleaning. I think that'll be present enough for Papa. Okay. I'll give you thirty cents. But think of something else, too, something for me to get Pa, huh?"

That was it! Carl on her side—well, at least not against her. And the thirty cents was as good as in her hand. "Please let Friday come in a hurry," she prayed. And then she added, "Saturday, too. I can't wait for Saturday!"

chapter 14

By the time Friday night came around, Pat was too nervous to sit still. Mrs. Marley felt her head.

"What's wrong with you, child?" she asked. "Maybe you're working too hard? Don't bother with the dishes. Go to bed."

"I'm all right, Mama. Honest. I just can't wait until Papa comes home," Pat said.

She helped defrost the refrigerator and washed the dishes. After that, her mother insisted she go to bed. All the arrangements for the party had been made. The neighbors had all been invited. Two floors of tenants were to come at one time. By six o'clock, according to Mrs. Marley's figures, the party would be over and Mr. Marley would be able to rest.

Pat tossed on her bed reviewing the plans, wondering who would be in the house at three o'clock when Sarah walked in. She heard Carl get into bed.

"Hey, quit bouncing around!" Carl whispered.

"I can't sleep," Pat whispered back.

Carl looked up at her and said knowingly, "Guilty conscience, I bet."

Pat leaned over the edge of her bed. "I have not! I've just been having bad dreams."

"Did you really invite Sarah?" He waited for her answer, then said, "No wonder you've got bad dreams. See policemen chasing you?"

Pat gulped. That was exactly what she had been dreaming. "It's awful," she admitted. "The cops keep coming toward me. They act as if I'm hiding someone."

Carl answered unsympathetically, "I'm glad you're worried. Better call the whole thing off now, while there's time."

"Then Papa won't get to see her. And I want her to go home and tell her mother about us."

"You're dreaming, kid," said Carl. "Take my advice and call it off."

"Then how will Mrs. Mellon ever let us be friends and visit each other?"

"How will this help?"

Pat sat up. "That's the trouble. Everybody talks. Talk. Talk. Talk. Integration! Who *does* anything about it?"

She crept under the covers and cried herself to sleep. That night in her dreams she never stopped running. Everyone was chasing her: policemen, Mr. Mellon, Mrs. Mellon, her mother—and even her father. She got up with circles under her eyes.

"I know something is wrong," her mother fretted as she served breakfast and beat up a chocolate cake at the same time.

Pat tried to swallow some of her oatmeal. Her mother kept stopping to look at her eyes.

"Is it something in school. Is it those two kids that are forever plaguing you—that Phyllis and that Eric?"

"No, Ma," Pat said, spooning cereal into her mouth with determination. That was the trouble with mothers, Pat thought, always worrying. "I'm just tired."

Mrs. Marley seemed to accept this explanation. She set the cake in the oven, sighing about all the work that had been done in preparation for Mr. Marley's home-coming. Every dish in the cupboard had been washed. Every closet had been cleaned.

Every finger mark had been scrubbed off the walls. Even the basement had been cleaned.

"Carl and Junior, you better get down to the store and deliver your orders. Make sure you come home for lunch. Papa will be dying to look at you," Mrs. Marley said as the two boys came up from the basement.

Pat listened to her mother run on as she got dressed. At ten o'clock, Mr. Oliver and Mr. Meadows would be downstairs waiting for her. The two men were going to the hospital with her. It would take both of them to carry Mr. Marley up the stairs in his chair. Her mother was obviously upset. She showed it in her rapid talk, in the way she picked things up and put them down as if she didn't know why she had picked them up in the first place.

"Don't worry, Mama. I'll clear up," Pat assured her.

"The cake isn't done. And see that Carl remembers to put on his brown shoes—I had them fixed. And. . . ."

"Mama, I'll take care of everything," Pat said, and threw her arms around her mother.

"Pat, I don't know what I'd have done without you these past few weeks," her mother said. "But I do know something is bothering you. All week I've felt it. If it weren't so late, I'd. . . ."

The car horn sounded and Pat helped her mother get her coat on. A small suitcase filled with her father's clothes stood ready at the door.

"Good-by," her mother called. "Good-by."

The twins and Ginny ran down the stairs ahead of her. All the way down, Pat could hear her mother cautioning them, "Be careful, now, not to run at Papa when he comes home. Don't all scream. Don't. . . ."

Pat put her hand over her rapidly beating heart. She knew how her mother was feeling. Would her father be changed? Would the house suddenly seemed cluttered to him? Noisy? Uncomfortable? Pat left the breakfast dishes in the sink and ran into the bedroom. She got the pillow. An extra pillow on the couch would make him more comfortable. And she'd get the bed sheets washed. Hospital linen must be gleaming white. She stripped the bed in record time.

"Pat!"

She heard her name and turned to see who had come into the room. It was Jo-Jo.

"Hi," she said.

"Where is everybody?" he asked cautiously.

She told him, and he came closer. "Pat, I have to talk to you."

She stopped stuffing sheets into the laundry bag. "What's up? Seems everybody's jumpy today."

"It's about Sarah."

Pat swallowed. She couldn't talk.

"Is she coming?"

Pat nodded.

Jo-Jo's face lengthened. "For sure?"

Pat nodded again.

"Gee. Lucy Mae and me—we met in the card store, and we decided. . . ."

"Haven't I enough on my mind without you bringing me gossip?"

Jo-Jo turned color and Pat felt tears sting her lids. She hadn't snapped at Jo-Jo in a long time.

"I'm sorry, Jo-Jo," she apologized. "I'm nervous about my father and about—you know what."

"That's what I want to tell you. Lucy Mae said what if Mrs. Mellon fires your mother. What if she finds out and gets sore and fires your mother?"

Pat sat down on the laundry bag. She hadn't thought about that before. "She couldn't be *that* mean. Jo-Jo, you don't think she'd do that?"

Jo-Jo shook his head uncertainly. He looked frightened. "No, she wouldn't do that, I guess. Not when your mother needs the money so bad and your father is just out of the hospital."

Pat nodded. Jo-Jo meant to be kind and helpful. There was no use in shouting at him or hurting his feelings. So, she held tightly to her tongue, got up, and began stuffing linens into the bag again.

"Don't fret, Jo-Jo. It'll be all right. Help me get this down to the laundromat." To comfort Jo-Jo as well as herself, she began to paint a picture of the events as she'd like them to be.

"I don't know why we're singing the blues. My father is coming home in an hour, and we're going to have a party. At three o'clock, Sarah is coming and then you'll see the best puppet show you've ever seen. My father will laugh till he cries."

Jo-Jo smiled. "That puppet show *is* funny."

"And, by Monday morning," continued Pat, "We'll be laughing at the way we were worrying this morning. Wait and see! Sarah will come with a note inviting us all to a party at *her* house!"

All the way to the laundromat, Pat continued her story. Once there, she stuffed laundry into the machine, put in her quarter, and watched the water spurt merrily into the tub. She nudged Jo-Jo. "Mrs. Mellon will give my mother a raise! Just you wait and see! And we'll be hopping with joy like soap bubbles."

Jo-Jo went home whistling.

Pat stayed at the laundromat. The machine went through its cycles and Pat felt better as she listened to the regular, predictable motion. Maybe her day

would be as predictable. The story she had told
Jo-Jo *must* come true.

The clothes were dry at twelve, and Pat went
flying home. She took it as a good omen that Mr.
Oliver's car wasn't at the door. She'd have time to
do the dishes, make the beds, and maybe get the
kids cleaned up, too. Surely no harm could come
of Sarah's visit. This was a good omen!

The door was open when she got there. The
little ones were screeching, "Papa's here."

Their dirty faces greeted her. She saw the sink
full of dishes. Beyond that, she saw the unmade bed.

"Papa?" she asked.

"Papa's here," Ginny trilled.

Pat came slowly into the kitchen, past the table.
She saw him on the couch. His arms were out-
spread.

"Papa," she repeated, and came slowly toward
him. Suddenly, omens didn't matter. It made no
difference that faces were dirty, or that the dishes
were undone. All she saw was her father's smile,
and the tears in his eyes. Sarah was forgotten.
Everything was forgotten.

"Papa," she cried, and threw herself alongside
the couch and into his arms.

chapter 15

Her father's laughter helped Pat stave off her panic. With his smile filling the room, it was easy to tell herself that he would understand her invitation to Sarah. Each time her mother's questioning gaze searched her face, Pat managed to bring up the necessary smile.

But, when the guests began coming and the time for Sarah's arrival drew closer, Pat couldn't sit still. She helped borrow chairs, filled bowls with candy and nuts, poured coffee, and, all the time, her eyes haunted the door.

"Go get Jo-Jo and Vanessa and Lucy Mae," her father urged her. "What are you hanging around listening to us dull old folks talk operations?"

She couldn't bear leaving. What if Sarah came while she was gone? She begged the twins to go and, for a change, as if they sensed her desperation, they ran off to get her friends without protest.

When her friends came, Pat gathered them on her bed.

To Vanessa's question, she answered, "Everythings wrong!" In one sentence, she told Vanessa, who already knew about Sarah, how she had invited the white girl to the party without telling her parents. "And the way my mother is looking at me, she'll guess about the fib to Sarah's mother the minute Sarah walks in here," Pat declared.

"Maybe I ought to wait at the bus stop and tell her to go home," Jo-Jo suggested. "I told you it was dangerous, didn't I?"

"This is no time to argue," said Lucy Mae sternly. "And Pat, it's no time for weakness. At first I didn't think you ought to coax Sarah to do something wrong. But now that you've done it, you can't be rude and send her home."

Vanessa wanted to know why Sarah was coming without permission. Pat went through all the complicated steps again.

"But," said Vanessa, "why didn't she tell her mother that your mother was her cleaning lady. That's the *most* important thing, I think."

"I told you," Pat declared.

Vanessa's face remained confused while Jo-Jo and Pat and Lucy Mae talked rapidly. Vanessa couldn't be convinced that Sarah could be a nice girl and refuse to admit to her mother that her best friend in class was a Negro.

"I wouldn't have a best friend that was afraid or ashamed to invite me to her house!" Vanessa said stubbornly.

"But that's why I did this!" Pat said hotly. "I want Sarah to go home and tell her mother all about us. She'll *have* to tell her today. She'll have to!"

"So. . . ." Vanessa looked from face to face. "Then, if that's it, what are you scared of? *If* she tells her mother, then your mother won't be angry. Or are you afraid she won't tell?"

"She'll tell," said Jo-Jo. "She's fun. I like her."

Lucy Mae refused to take such an argument seriously. "We all like her and she is fun. But I agree with Vanessa. Does that show that Sarah *has* to tell her mother about today? Or does it show she *will* tell?"

Pat shook her head. "Lucy Mae, you know Sarah can't keep a secret. What ever she thinks about, she talks about."

"Then how come she didn't tell her mother about

your mother being her cleaning lady?" Vanessa asked with unrelenting logic.

"Ask her when she comes," said Pat calmly. Defending Sarah made her fears seem less real. As long as she could talk about Sarah's visit with someone, she felt more at ease.

Just then, Mrs. Oliver, who had come to help Mrs. Marley serve, came into the bedroom carrying a bowl of potato chips. "Knock, knock," she said gaily. "The talk here is as grown-up as it is in the living room—and much quieter. Are you gossiping about your friends or talking about your school?"

She stood near the bunk bed for an instant and Pat nodded. "In a way we are, Mrs. Oliver. We want to know how we can make the mothers get to know us if they never invite us to their houses. *We* know the white kids. But their parents don't know anything about us at all."

"That's a problem the P.T.A. is tackling," Mrs. Oliver answered. "Mrs. Bondy. . . ."

"Debby's mother?" Pat interrupted.

"Yes, Deborah's mother," Mrs. Oliver confirmed. "Mrs. Bondy invited the program committee to her house. That's the committee I'm on, and the topic of discussion is going to be just what you are interested in."

"Getting us invited to white childrens' houses?" Lucy Mae asked.

Pat whooped with delight.

In the other room, Mr. Marley heard the excited cries from the bedroom and called out, "What's going on in there?"

Mrs. Oliver and the children came out and a discussion of the committee's problem began in earnest.

"Everyone is interested in integration these days!" Lucy Mae said to Vanessa as they walked into the other room.

Mrs. Oliver first told about her committee. Pat listened attentively. Mrs. Mellon's name was mentioned, too. She hadn't known that Mrs. Oliver knew Sarah's mother.

Mrs. Meadows interrupted Mrs. Oliver's story. She turned to Pat's mother. "That Mrs. Mellon is a strange woman. Don't you think so?"

Pat watched her mother carefully. She knew her mother usually kept quiet about her feelings, even when asked a direct question. Jobs were jobs, not love affairs, her mother would say. Mrs. Marley rarely mentioned the Mellons. But now she was being asked a direct question in front of an audience.

"Yes, she's strange. But I think she's a good woman. She tries to be fair."

"But I hated to work for her," Mrs. Meadows said. "She treated me just like a servant."

Pat squirmed, and her father caught her eye. "Say, what are we boring our young ones for?" he said. "Talk about something they can understand. They'll have time enough for such talk when they get to be our age." He beckoned Pat to his side. "Tell these people about your new class."

He held her hand as she talked. To Mr. Meadows, he winked and said, "You and I were scared to let our kids go across town. Remember? The women had to talk us into it. But look at our kids now! Both of them getting good marks. No letters from the teachers—except an invitation to come to a P.T.A. meeting and see them perform in some fancy puppet show." He patted Pat's head.

Pat wanted to hear more about Mrs. Mellon, but her curiosity had to be curbed. Mr. Edwards, from the first floor, wanted to know how it happened that her marks had improved in this school. Mr. Marley joined him in the question.

Pat took her eyes from Mrs. Oliver, and looked at her shoes. How could she explain what she didn't quite understand herself?

Lucy Mae tried to answer for her. "We ride for half an hour on the bus. We study while we ride."

Jo-Jo shook his head. "That's not all. I know I never used to study. But that was because the teacher always used to look at us as if she didn't expect us to know the answers. So, I never cared."

Vanessa giggled. "Remember Mrs. Dillon? She'd put work on the board and if we asked her how to do it, she used to say, 'If you'd listen, you'd know without asking.'"

Jo-Jo blew his cheeks out at the memory. "Only, even if we listened, she didn't tell us. If you asked a question, she thought you were being fresh. Remember, Pat?"

Pat forced her thoughts away from Sarah and Mrs. Mellon. Her mother was looking at her as if expecting some profound truth. Pat looked around the room and spoke. "Jo-Jo is right. Mrs. Klein, my teacher, looks as if she expects us to know the answers. When we ask questions, she listens to us and explains until we understand."

Then Pat made Jo-Jo and Lucy Mae and Vanessa come around in a circle and she stepped to the front of the group. Jo-Jo grinned. "Just like Mrs. Klein," he whispered to the grownups.

Pat asked, "How much does it cost to buy four pairs of socks if each pair costs a quarter?"

Lucy Mae gave the wrong answer on purpose, and giggled. Pat stepped to her side. "Who laughed? Who in this room is so smart, he can afford to laugh at anyone else's mistake? Everyone here, including *me* has lots to learn. This is something Lucy Mae needs to learn. And she'll learn it right now!"

The grownups burst out into laughter. Mr. Marley laughed loudest and longest. "What a girl," he kept saying. "What a girl."

The performance was over, but the grownups persisted in their questioning. Mrs. Oliver helped to explain the changes. "There is special coaching. Mrs. Klein does her own, but then, she is a dedicated teacher. Not all the teachers are as good as she is."

Pat recalled the number of times Mrs. Klein stood at her side, watching her work. "She stops me before I make mistakes. Sometimes she makes me draw pictures of examples. Sometimes she has me use sticks or discs."

"And in spelling, she plays games with the words," Jo-Jo said. "She plays lots of games. It isn't like learning."

"Yet, you *do* learn," said Mrs. Oliver.

"I wish I could go," Vanessa said, after the talk died down. Then she stopped. "No, I don't," she said vehemently. "Jo-Jo, you told me that the reason you study is that you're scared stiff someone is going to call you an ape if you make a mistake."

Jo-Jo admitted it was the truth, and the grownups took sides. Some said that a little honest fright was a good thing. Others said they'd rather stay close at home and learn less of hate and fear.

The argument was going strong and Pat found an opportunity to move close to Mrs. Oliver. "Were you talking about Sarah Mellon's mother before? Do you think Sarah's mother hates us?"

Mrs. Oliver looked startled. "She's—polite," Mrs. Oliver said hesitantly. "Pat, you must understand that integration is a new thing for some people. Now, Mrs. Bondy is ready to accept changes. She sees that they are past due. Mrs. Mellon may see that, too, but she's not quite ready."

Pat almost told Mrs. Oliver then. She started to say, "I'm going to help Mrs. Mellon understand." But her mother interrupted with the suggestion that she take her friends into the kitchen and serve them some cake and milk.

"And you leave integration and making Mrs. Mellon understand to the grownups," Mrs. Marley concluded with a special nod for Mrs. Oliver.

That was when the downstairs doorbell rang and every eye turned to the door. Who would be ringing downstairs? Everyone except the Olivers lived in the building. And the Olivers were already here.

Pat met three pairs of eyes before she met her mother's.

"I'll go down and see," said Pat quietly.

"Me, too," Jo-Jo, Lucy Mae, and Vanessa said in turn.

Mrs. Marley looked at Pat, suddenly knowing. "Pat, you didn't?"

Pat's heart beat frantically. She made her eyes say all the things she hoped for and, as her mother's face grew longer and longer in the silence, she came close to her mother and whispered, "I'm sorry. I thought . . . for Papa. . . ."

Her mother looked toward the couch. Her father's laughter greeted her questioning eyes. "Come and sit near me," he called, and Mrs. Marley nodded. Pat touched the place on her mother's cheek where a pulse had begun to beat unevenly.

"I'm sorry, Mama."

A sigh was her only answer. "Go get her, Pat," her mother said, after what seemed forever. "I'll have to get her home right away."

Mrs. Marley walked them to the door. The four children followed after her. Pat went out the door first and led the way to the stairs. She heard her mother pray softly, "Forgive the child and don't let anything awful happen. Let me get that white child home safely. And forgive my dark one!"

Pat whispered to the other children, "She's going to send Sarah right home. What will Sarah say?"

But no one could answer her.

chapter 16

Pat raced down the stairs two at a time. The others were right behind her. Pat's heart kept a loud rhythm that seemed to say, "What will Sarah say —what will Sarah say."

But it wasn't only Sarah who waited for them at the front door. There was someone else with her.

"Debby! Sarah!" Pat cried.

The girls threw their arms around one another. Vanessa was introduced. And then, Jo-Jo said sadly, "Gee, and Mrs. Marley is going to make you go right home."

"You're kidding!" Sarah said loudly.

Pat nodded and Sarah hopped up and down.

"You mean we came all this way for *nothing?*"

"I don't mind," Debby murmured. "I just came to tell you I'm glad your father is home."

Pat looked right into Debby's eyes. Debby was serious! She had come all this way, without even being asked, just to. . . . "Did you really come just to tell me?" Pat asked. It was unbelievable. And then she remembered, with a pang, all the begging she had done to convince Sarah to make the trip.

Debby nodded.

"Yes," Sarah answered for her, "that's exactly why she came. She said she wished she could tell you and I said she ought to come, and. . . ." Sarah giggled. Then she went on between giggles, "It made things easy. We didn't have to tell a lie. I said I was going with Debby and Debby said she was going with me, and we both told the truth!" She laughed louder. "Only we didn't say where!"

Pat came closer to Debby. She didn't laugh with the others. She stared at Debby. Except for her family, no one had ever taken such a risk for her sake. Not even Jo-Jo. He had failed her on that very important first day of school.

"Why did you do it? Why do you care about me?"

Debby blushed but met her eyes. "Because you never called me a tattletale or any of those names. You were scared like I was when you first came.

And I—I liked other things about you. You stick up for your friends and things like that!"

Pat's chest began to swell to enormous proportions. Protectively, she put her arm around Debby. "Come on up. I guess my mother wants to see you and explain—even if she is nervous about your coming."

Pat walked between Sarah and Debby, thinking of the wonder of what had happened. "A *white* girl likes me well enough to come across town to tell me she's glad about my father! And puppets had nothing to do with that friendship."

She turned to Debby, "If you tell your mother, and if your mother gives you permission, you could come here any time," Pat said.

"I'm going to tell her as soon as I get home," Debby said.

Pat put her head back and looked up at the ceiling. She took a deep breath and filled her lungs. In the time it took her to do that, she had made up her mind.

"I'm not going to *let* my mother send you home," she said. "You and Debby took a chance coming here. Sarah's mother would. . . ."

"Flip! And then I'd never hear the end of it," Sarah interrupted.

Pat nodded. "So, I'm going to *make* my mother let you come in. I'm going to make *sure* my father isn't worried. Let's go."

Her arms tightened around Debby and Sarah, as they came up the five flights.

"You sure have good friends," Vanessa said to Lucy Mae.

Lucy Mae grinned. "It's Pat who makes them. She's what Debby said—loyal and kind."

Pat heard it and her ears tingled. She wanted to look back and see Lucy Mae's face.

Both Debby and Sarah chimed in when Lucy Mae finished. "And how!"

"Wait'll you see her puppet show," Sarah added. "It's tops!"

Modestly, Pat said, "It's as much yours as mine."

"That's why it's tops!" said Sarah, and they all giggled.

Mrs. Marley was waiting at the door. She stepped into the hall as soon as the group reached the landing.

"Shhh," Pat begged.

But Mrs. Marley paid no attention. "Please excuse me, Sarah," she said, as if she had a speech already memorized. "But unless your mother gave you permission to be here, I've asked Mrs. Oliver to drive you home. You must forgive us, but Mr. Marley can't be. . . ."

"Good afternoon, Mrs. Marley," said Debby. Mrs. Marley hadn't seen her in the darkness of the hall.

With new appreciation, Pat saw the forthright thrust of Debby's chin.

"Ma," Pat said with a new dignity, "I'm sorry I made Sarah tell her mother a lie. I'm sorry I didn't tell you. I'm sorry you worried. But Mama," Pat's voice held all the wonder she felt. "Mama, Debby came all on her own. I didn't beg her to come like I begged Sarah. I didn't even *ask* her. She *wanted* to come to tell us how glad she is about Papa being home. Please, Mama, can't my friends come in so Papa can see them? I want everybody to see my friends. Please, Mama."

Mrs. Marley took Debby's hand. "Did you, Deborah? Did you want to tell us that? How lovely." Then Mrs. Marley shook her head. "But you didn't tell *your* mother," she said, looking hopefully at Debby. *"Did* you?"

Debby shook her head.

Mrs. Marley's mouth set in a hard line.

Debby said hurriedly, "But I'm going to tell my mother the second I get home."

Pat saw the indecision in her mother's eyes. "Please, Ma, it won't worry Papa. We'll do the puppet show. He'll laugh. And then we'll eat as fast as we can and the girls will go home."

"If you give me thirty cents more," Sarah said with a grin. "All we had was thirty cents, and thirty of it is gone."

Mrs. Marley laughed. "Sarah, you're always joking. We'll worry about that trip home in a little while. Right now, you girls had better not say anything to worry Mr. Marley. He's been sick a long time."

Pat kissed her mother. They were in! She led the girls into the living room with a dip and a bow. "Ladies and gentlemen," she announced to the third and second floor neighbors, "*and* Mr. Marley! I want you to meet my friends Sarah and Debby."

Mr. Marley looked as if the sun had risen behind his eyes. He greeted the girls as Pat dreamed he would. "Just the honor of your coming to visit would make a broken hip worth-while," he said with a grin. "Mama, the girls would probably like hot chocolate or soda."

After the soda, it was puppet show time. Carl and Junior set up two chairs between the living room and the bedroom. Lucy Mae and Vanessa held up a sheet for the curtain, lowering it when the show began, to hide the two puppeteers.

Pat took the puppets out of the bag. The Negro puppet, Pamela, had never looked so lovely. She smoothed the puppet's dress into soft folds. Sarah was watching her.

"Pamela really does look like you," she said to Pat. "Look in the mirror!"

It was good to hear Sarah say that, even if it wasn't really true. Except for the puppet's color, Pat felt she and Pamela had nothing in common. Pamela had long, wavy hair. Pat had short braids.

Debby followed Pat's gaze. "Except for the hair," she said, "Pamela *does* look like you."

With a quick intake of breath, Pat hid her delight. She promised to look at herself in the mirror when everyone else had left. She'd always avoided that before.

She watched Sarah slip her fingers into Pamela's sleeve-dress.

Then, their arms went up over the tops of the chairs. The play had started.

Sarah whispered to Pat, "Let's go, girl! This is our first grown-up audience. I sure hope they like it!"

Pat made sure they would. Her fingers seemed untiring. They dangled Sar-occhio on the cart, they dangled her from a kite, they looped her and they bounced her in and out of make-believe trees. Every time Sar-occhio cried, Pat put every ounce of herself in those cries. Every time Sar-occhio laughed, Pat made sure the entire room echoed with laughter.

"Do some more," the twins yelled, when the curtain came down on Sar-occhio clinging passionately to Pamela and crying, "You saved me. You saved me. Thank you. Thank you."

Mrs. Marley wiped tears from her eyes. Mr. Marley held his arms open. "Pat. Sarah. I never saw such a show. You two are wonderful. He smiled at Lucy Mae and Debby and Vanessa and Jo-Jo. "Couldn't do without the stage people, either!"

"Bring the puppets out," Mrs. Meadows called. "What beautiful puppets!"

"They are beautiful," said Mr. Marley. "It's as good as anything in the movies." He picked up Pamela and turned the puppet around and around. "I didn't think you'd ever do it," he exclaimed. "Before this new school business, you were crying that you couldn't be Negro and be beautiful. You couldn't be Negro and be good. Now look at that!" He turned the black puppet every which way.

Pat and Sarah stared at him. It suddenly dawned on Pat that he—and probably the others, too—thought that Pat had made the Negro puppet. Pat started to protest.

"You have it wrong, Papa. . . ."

Mr. Marley chuckled. "I probably do. But then, I can't get my big old fingers into those tiny sleeves."

"No, papa," Pat said, stifling a giggle. He looked

funny and everyone was laughing at the joke. Suddenly Pat laughed, too. What difference did it make who had made the black puppet? It was a fine puppet and Sar-occhio was a fine puppet. Everyone was praising both of them.

She poked Sarah and shook her head. Sarah wouldn't give the secret away. Black or white, what difference did it make? Nice people were nice no matter what color they were. She winked at Sarah and Debby. The children burst out laughing. The grownups laughed, too, not even realizing what the joke was.

Later, after Mrs. Oliver had driven the two girls home, Pat curled up by her father's side. The day's activities had tired him out and he was fast asleep on the couch. Pat sat on the floor, her chin resting on her knees, her back against the sofa.

The room was dark. The only light was from the kitchen, where her mother was clearing away the last of the party things.

Pat held her hand up in the dark. She could barely see its outline, and she remembered doing the same thing once before, during the summer. How frightened she had been then. How silly it seemed now. It didn't matter that she couldn't *see* her hand. After all, she *knew* it was there.

"Papa?" she whispered.

Only a gentle snore answered her.

"Papa?" she whispered again. "I'm glad you made me go across town to school. I made a lot of new friends." She shut her eyes and continued thoughtfully. "Can you have half a friend?" When there was no answer, she answered herself. "Sarah is half a friend because we can only be friends in school. I feel sad about Sarah." Then she opened her eyes. Her father had turned over.

"But I have *three* and a half friends!" Pat spoke louder. She counted on her fingers. "Jo-Jo's my friend. He's the oldest one. Then there's the ones I made across town: Lucy Mae, even though she lives just across the street, Debby, and my *school* friend, Sarah. Isn't that a lot?"

Her father turned over heavily, sighed, and patted her on the head.

Pat hugged herself. It didn't matter if he had heard what she had said. Being so black hadn't stopped her from making friends. It hadn't kept her from learning. She was happy and her father knew it. And that was what counted most of all.

About the Author

Betty Baum, a teacher trained in the All-Day Neighborhood School Program in New York City, is a graduate of Hunter College. Though she has written many articles and short stories before, PATRICIA CROSSES TOWN is her first book. Mrs. Baum, a mother and grandmother, lives in Jamaica, Long Island.

A NOTE ON THE TYPE

This book is set in Granjon, a type named in compliment to Robert Granjon, but neither a copy of a classic face nor an entirely original creation. George W. Jones drew the basic design for this type from classic sources, but deviated from his model to profit by the intervening centuries of experience and progress. This type is based primarily upon the type used by Claude Garamond (1510–61) in his beautiful French books, and more closely resembles Garamond's own than do any of the various modern types that bear his name.

Robert Granjon began his career as type-cutter in 1523. The boldest and most original designer of his time, he was one of the first to practice the trade of type-founder apart from that of printer.